JOHNNY THE POOKIE

Iain Price

Pen Press Publishers Ltd

Published in Great Britain by
Pen Press Publishers Ltd
39–41, North Road
Islington
London N7 9DP

ISBN 1-905203-15-2

Cover design by Jacqueline Abromeit

Printed and bound in Great Britain by
Cpod, Trowbridge, Wiltshire

About the Author

Iain was born in Bewdley, Worcestershire in 1967. He was educated and spent most of his childhood in the nearby town of Bromsgrove. Having graduated from Exeter University in 1989 with a degree in Economics & Statistics, Iain worked in IT in Birmingham where he met his wife, a native of Islandeady, County Mayo. They married in 1994 and moved to Islandeady in 1997, where they now live on a farm with their two young children.

Acknowledgements

The author would like to acknowledge the support and understanding of all his friends and relatives over the years. In particular he would like to thank his wife for her patience, loyalty and constant encouragement.
The author also acknowledges that despite his pessimism in 2003 when writing this text, Mayo Football team proved both he and many others wrong by winning the Connaught Championship and making the All Ireland Final. Congratulations and thanks to them for a memorable year. Hopefully they will emulate the success of the Mayo Ladies in the next few years and win the Final.

Contents

Prologue

Changing Seasons

It is a mistake to think that anything can happen at Halloween. The truth is that anything can happen at any time.

Now, such a sentence as this is usually followed by the words 'within reason'. This is strange in itself, because, quite often, the things that do happen to us are not what we would reasonably expect. It is only with hindsight, looking back at our experiences, that we make enough sense of events in our lives to allow that they are 'within reason'. That is to say, within the definition of reason that exists, ever changing, in our minds.

Sometimes this requires no small amount of sub-conscious editing on our part. We need to make our memories fit comfortably into our own world-view. And we need to protect ourselves from the trauma of having that view challenged, or even obliterated. But sometimes no amount of editing will suffice.

Some experiences are just too far beyond the comfort-zone of our self-defined reason for us to contend with. And when this happens, it can drive some people mad. Others may cope by throwing away their world-view and starting again. Though perhaps when we see them, we think that they too are mad.

Remarkably though, when confronted with such a challenge, one that contradicts all perceived reason, most people do survive. They survive because the human mind is capable of suspending and redefining reality, expanding its world-view and accepting truths that it cannot comprehend. It is a survival technique that allows for flexible boundaries, to contain and protect a different reason, one that is open to new and almost limitless possibilities. This survival technique has a well-known name – imagination.

Children in particular are capable of employing this survival technique frequently and favourably. From the earliest age their world-view constantly changes and their reason continually develops. This often requires massive leaps, not just of reason, but also of imagination, and faith.

It is not until adulthood that we have become confined and conditioned by those artificial boundaries and prejudices of the mind that are created by an organised society. It is a reality that is eventually imprinted upon us like a canvas until we learn to reinforce it, justify it, and then promote it ourselves. For a child, the imagination is stronger, the boundaries less well defined, the canvas more incomplete.

It was for this reason that Séamus Moran survived this story and remained, for the most part, an ordinary boy. It is a story where the events that take place followed the festival that used to be known in Séamus's country as *Samhain*, a time of changing seasons and a time of remembering those that have departed. It is a time also where the human mind recalls from the past other beliefs and other possibilities that today lie outside the realms of our reason. The story begins at Halloween, not because it has to, but perhaps because it is a time when it is easier to remember that anything really is possible after all.

Chapter 1

A Strange Visitor

The morning was as ordinary as they come.

"You look like Johnny the Pookie!" said Mrs Moran.

Séamus tucked his vest in and hurried past his mother to his room so that now his sister got his mother's attention.

"And you look like Johnny the Pookie's sister!"

Sinéad just smiled at her. Most corrections got this disarming response from Sinéad. Being the youngest and being a girl she usually got away with it.

This time it worked and a smile now appeared on Mrs Moran's face.

"Straighten yoursells up before ye head outside again," she commanded.

Séamus was soon on his way past Mrs Moran once more, carrying a hurley, having made himself more presentable and removed some of the more obvious dirt and grass stains from his bare knees. Sinéad stayed indoors this time and, without realising it, Mrs Moran found herself tidying her up and brushing her hair for her.

"Now. You look a bit less of a gibble," she pronounced and Sinéad headed off to the dining room to carry on with one of her favourite jigsaws. It was the third one she had done so far today.

Pookies and Gibbles. That's what the Moran children were referred to by their parents when they did or said anything daft, or appeared looking too dishevelled or dirty to escape unnoticed. It was only a mild admonition though. If they were really bold, no additional label would be applied, just their names enunciated in the sternest tone.

That had happened once or twice this morning, the first morning of the half-term holiday after Halloween at the weekend. Séamus and Sinéad went to Scoil Raifteirí, a Gaelscoil in Castlebar. This was an Irish-speaking school a few miles from their house that was situated in the countryside, about halfway between the towns of Westport and Castlebar, in County Mayo in the West of Ireland. That was why Séamus had a hurley, or a *camán*, a stick for playing the Irish game of hurling, something he enjoyed at home and at school.

The children lived in the little village of Dooleen, the farthest in of half a dozen houses, in a stone cottage on top of a hill overlooking the Dooleen Lakes. Two other houses in the village were owned by relatives, one by an aunt and another by an uncle and his wife, the aunt and uncle being a sister and a brother of their mother.

Their father was originally from Stoneybatter in Dublin, and he still worked in Dublin, Ireland's capital city. They had dropped him off at the train at Westport station on Sunday evening as usual and would not see him again until Friday evening when he got the train back home.

When they had got home on Sunday evening Séamus and Sinéad had lit the candle in the pumpkin face that they had made together for Halloween. Sinéad had gasped as if she saw something frightening in the face, but she recovered her composure and said nothing to her brother other than the one word – "Interesting." Then, after she had checked the cattle, their mother had read them a scary story.

The nights were closing in again, otherwise Séamus may well have been sent to check the cattle himself, as he was now twelve, starting his penultimate year in the school. Sinéad, two years younger, could also have been dispatched to perform the duty, being generally energetic and afraid of nothing, but she was content for others to have the honour once most of the blackberries were gone off the bushes.

There were few berries left now, although more than you would get in most other places. With all the rain and wind in the West of Ireland, most plants flowered late, so that even after the end of October, you could still get a few late batches of berries for a blackberry pie. The Morans normally did this, even though the old local sayings held that blackberries should not be touched after Halloween, as the Pooka would have marred them.

"Dinner in an hour," said Mrs Moran as Séamus exited via the front door.

"*Ceart go leor*," was the response from Séamus.

This means 'okay' to the likes of you and me who don't know too much Irish, and it is worth noting at this point that the Moran household could be quite a bamboozling place to be in this regard, especially when Mr Moran was working away. He did not have much Irish himself, only *coupla focal,* a few words, as they would say in Ireland. But Mrs Moran was fluent, as were her parents, and the two children were far from being beginners after spending a few years in the Gaelscoil.

As a result, they would often lapse into a kind of random mixture of English and Irish sentences when Mr Moran was away in Dublin, easily going from one to the other without even noticing. It is therefore safe to assume that half at least of what is recorded here of their conversation was *as Gailge* (in Irish), though for ease of reading, and no less ease of recording, it will be written in the text here mostly in the manner that you and I are more familiar with: that's *as Béarla* (in English).

Séamus closed the door and turned towards the view of the Reek, County Mayo's famous mountain of pilgrimage, Croagh Patrick, ready to charge around the garden in his imaginary game. He was playing for Kilkenny, the Cats, in an All Ireland Hurling final. He would have preferred to play for Mayo, of course, but they were more of a footballing county, Gaelic Football that is, and did not have much hope of reaching a final in the hurling, even in his imagination. Come to think of it, they did not have much chance of reaching a final in the football in recent years either; the best he could imagine was victory in the Connaught final over Galway, hopefully soon.

Sometimes he fancied himself too old for this kind of thing, but up on the top of the hill in the garden and surrounding fields where no one could see him, he had decided to give in to his imagination and did not worry about whether he was engaged in childish activities. Having to be sensible in school five days a week was quite enough for now – he was on holiday and it was time to be a full forward and enjoy himself. He might play at being Cúchulainn also, the Celtic hero originally called Setanta, who got the name of Culann's hound after he slew the animal with his *sliotar*, the small hard ball used in hurling, and agreed to take the animal's place guarding Culann's land until he had trained a new dog. Séamus had a dog called Setanta, and he looked around for him as he moved away from the front door, *camán* and *sliotar* now in either hand.

He stopped dead in his tracks though as he turned towards the garden. There he saw an old man on his right, colourfully dressed, and stooped over a heavy walking stick, more like a cudgel or a shillelagh.

The old man half stood and half leaned on the low garden wall to the front of the house. He wore black, scruffy, baggy trousers and large black boots, but his shirt was a bright yellow and his waistcoat a disastrous, luminous green. The effect was that the attention was taken away from his face, which was half shaded by a battered black hat, crumpled like a concertina. Black and grey bushy hair emerged on either side and underneath the ancient headwear. This made it difficult enough to see his features clearly anyway, even if you had not already been too dazzled by his upper garments.

He was clean-shaven at least, although his face had a grimy and sunburnt look where it was visible, the left side slightly twisted by the fact that the man sported an old small clay pipe in his mouth. Séamus thought it was the sort that his great grandfather may have smoked once upon a time.

"Mummy's in the house," said Séamus automatically whilst he took in the sight of the strange old man, moving away in the direction of the fields where he intended to play out his games.

"I used to live in this house once," replied the old man.

His voice was clear and merry and not at all what Séamus had expected. The old man's eyes seemed to light up in a grin when he spoke, raising his head so Séamus could see beneath the rim of his hat.

All at once Séamus felt more at ease and strangely interested in the man, despite his wish to be on his way. More to the point, the content of the man's speech had arrested Séamus. Used to live here?

"What do you mean?" he said, "This is a new house – I mean it's only a few years old. Mummy and Daddy had it built."

"The stone in this house is the stone from the old house, over yonder field," said the old man. He inclined his head towards where the old ruined farmhouse had once stood not far away.

"'Tis the same house to me."

Séamus frowned and knitted his brow. He remembered snippets of conversation that his parents and grandparents had spoken about the history of the village, and this farm in particular.

"But the Durkins used to live there didn't they – and aren't they all dead for years? Did you live with them for a time perhaps?"

This drew a slight chuckle from the old man. He withdrew the pipe from his mouth and gave Séamus a broad grin.

"No, no Séamus-in" he said, "I was well before their time. But *sin sceal eile* as they say," meaning that that's another story.

He paused for a second. "Now Séamus," he continued fixing Séamus with a stare, the right eye doing all the work as the left of the face was screwed up again in concentration, "you'll help an old neighbour won't you?"

Séamus, in the moment that he had to think and take in what was said and what was asked, was suddenly flustered and at a loss for words. Something of the friendly nature of the old man had gone. The situation somehow seemed more awkward, even sinister. He felt a kind of shiver come over him as if a cloud had passed overhead, between him and the consolation of the November sun.

Who was this strange visitor? He clearly could not be from the old farmhouse before the time of the Durkins – that was preposterous. He'd have to be at least a hundred and fifty if that were the case. And what help was he expecting from a twelve-year-old boy? If the old man wanted to speak to someone it should be his mother.

So, feeling distinctly uneasy now, Séamus turned around and called, "Mummy! Visitor!" Then he added over his shoulder, without glancing at the man, "Mummy will be out soon," and so saying, moved quickly in the direction of the fields again. He was stopped almost immediately however, as a deep, growling reply came from behind him.

"I expected better hospitality than that!"

It was said in such a way that it almost turned Séamus's blood to ice. It made him feel compelled to turn to face the old man once more, apologise, say that he hadn't meant any offence, that he thought the man should talk to an adult if he needed assistance. But no words came out of his mouth when he turned.

The old man was gone.

Mrs Moran came to the door, wiping her hands on her apron. "Yes, Séamus," she said, "a visitor did you say?"

"An... an old man..." said Séamus looking about him mystified, "but he seems to have gone."

7

"Pretty quick on his feet then, for an old man," said Mrs Moran in a severe tone, "if he's out of sight in the time it took me to get to the porch."

"But Mummy…"

"Look, Séamus," continued his mother, "I'll talk to you a bit later, but I'm busy with chores at the moment. Just play on your own for a bit eh?"

"There was a man!" insisted Séamus earnestly.

"Yes, dear," sighed Mrs Moran with a sympathetic and resigned look on her face, "Johnny the Pookie I expect."

She turned and closed the door and left Séamus outside looking about him, still very puzzled and also annoyed. His mother had clearly put the incident down to his imagination or to mischief. He was twelve for goodness sake.

"Dinner in fifty minutes!" came the shout from indoors.

Séamus looked at his *camán* and shrugged his shoulders. He headed off at last for the fields to score some points, and maybe a goal, and to find his dog. Silly old man – probably slipped off the wall and sneaked off from behind the bushes, too embarrassed to say anything, Séamus decided.

At the back of his mind though, he wasn't convinced.

Chapter 2

What Granny had to say

Tuesday morning was clear and dry so Séamus decided to walk down the old bog road with the dog. The road began next to the Morans' house and carried on winding for a mile or so over an old narrow bridge, crossing a small river, until it emerged at another small village, called Bolnacorrishan, nestling between two small lakes. Séamus did not walk that far though, but turned to his left, a couple of hundred yards after the bridge, and went to explore around the bog.

He had spent many an hour there in the summer with his parents and his sister helping to foot the turf (peat for the range and the open fire) and then bag it for bringing home once it was dry enough. But he preferred to be in the bog as it was now, when he was on his own or just with Setanta. There were lots of dips and pools and bushes to hide behind and Séamus had many secret hideouts in the bog, and on the route to it, which played a role in many of his imaginary games.

Setanta, a small black Labrador cross, loved the bog as well, and went charging around following various scents, not caring about getting wet and smelly in the pools, nor in the trenches where the turf had been cut. Séamus on the other hand had to take a care not to get too filthy or it would spell trouble for him.

After a while, a long while it seemed running around with Setanta and checking various old and potentially new dens, Séamus picked up a stray sod of turf – there were always a few that either got missed or were too wet and not worth bringing home when the turf was collected – and sauntered back towards the entrance to the bog. Perched on an old white tree stump, bleached by the acidity of the bog, a wren watched both him and Setanta from a short distance away.

Séamus marvelled that it did not take flight in such close proximity to people, not to mention a medium-sized dog that had just been chasing anything that moved. He recalled now that he had caught sight of it, or another wren, a couple of times on his walk down to the bog and thought it odd. Wrens in his experience were normally shy of people and you only tended to get a good look at these small birds in winter when the food was much more scarce.

Séamus did his best to distract Setanta at this point, fearing the dog would make a leap for the bird, maybe even catch it at this range if he noticed it. Then a strange thing happened. Setanta, turning to face the bird, stood still with his hackles raised and began to snarl and bark at the creature, edging forward slightly rather than in his usual fearless and frenzied canter.

"Setanta, stop – come here!" shouted Séamus and made a grab for the dog's collar.

He was feeling puzzled by the dog's tardiness in attack, but was glad of the unexpected opportunity to intervene. The attempt to restrain him only seemed to bring Setanta back to his usual self though, and, too quick for Séamus, he sprang in the direction of the tree stump. Séamus slipped to his knees in a failed lunge at the hound, and then looked up expecting to see feathers flying or Setanta in hot pursuit of a terrified wren. But all he saw was a confused looking dog, an empty tree stump, and his filthy trousers.

The bird must have taken flight and the dog had not seen where it went, thought Séamus, as he busily tried to make the best of his condition, brushing off as much dirt and heather from his clothing as possible. At least that was the only sensible conclusion he could come to, although, for some reason, thoughts of yesterday's encounter with the strange old man suddenly came into his mind and Séamus felt troubled. He decided he would speak to Granny about it when they drove over to Kilagan that afternoon. Granny knew everyone and their history in every part of the parish, and she knew about the countryside. She would make sense of it all, he was sure.

It was after dinner when, at last, the Moran household headed on the short journey from Dooleen to Kilagan. The excursion involved driving down the length of the narrow, hilly and windy Dooleen road for just over a mile until it joined the main Westport to Castlebar road. A turn right on to the road to head towards Westport was followed almost immediately by a turn left under a railway arch that looked so narrow that it could not possibly be a road at all. In fact, before the Community Council had recently commissioned signposts for the village names in the parish of Islandeady, holiday-goers had frequently treated it as a lay-by. They would stop there, maybe to have a picnic or a rest in front of the arch, only to be politely (and sometimes impolitely) asked to move after a little while by a Kilagan villager wishing to get to or from his home. It was a mile or so again along the Kilagan road where Mrs Moran's parents lived on their own farm, rather larger than the farm on Dooleen hill. Séamus and Sinéad always enjoyed their trips to their grandparents' house. The old pair were great craic, as they would say, meaning that they were a lot of fun!

After a while Granddad went to check the cattle, some distance away over his fields, and Mrs Moran and Sinéad went along with him for the walk. Granny stayed to make some tea on the range and prepare some slices of cake for their return. She was surprised that Séamus stayed with her rather than take the opportunity to go running over more fields. Séamus always liked to run and Granny wondered if he was a little under the weather.

So she asked him, in Irish of course, if there was any news and if he was okay. And Séamus answered her, in Irish of course, so that they soon got onto the topic of Séamus's recent encounters with the strange old man and the wren.

Normally, it would be very difficult to get Granny to sit down or stand still for very long, but this seemed to be enough to stop her in her tracks. She ceased to go about her chores with a concerned expression.

"That's bad, that's bad," she said, looking nervously at Séamus and leaning now against the living room table. Séamus now bore a downcast look, as clearly the explanation was not to be the words of comfort he had hoped for and expected.

"What is it, Granny – what's wrong?"

"Pooka," she declared. "Or the Sidhe," she pronounced this 'shee', "Leprechauns, Banshees, Faery Folk, call them what you will. Male or female, man or beast, it's the same thing – spirits from the past, powerful creatures from the Otherworld. They can be good or bad, and if you've upset one then there's sure to be trouble. Oh Jesus, Mary and Joseph, there's sure to be trouble!" and she crossed herself at least three times as she said all this.

So earnestly had she spoken, in almost a whisper, as if she were afraid of being overheard, that Séamus now felt really scared. He leapt to his feet from the chair, with tears in his eyes, and asserted to his grandmother, "But I didn't do anything!"

The look of terror on her grandson's face and the pleading in his voice brought his grandmother back to herself. She straightened herself up and pulled Séamus into her apron giving him a tight hug.

"There there, Séamus-in," she said, "It may not be so bad, it was just a misunderstanding wasn't it? And sure, the wren did you no harm? You're only a child, and it would be a miserable Pookie that bothered to do you any mischief!"

She stroked Séamus's head as she spoke with a look of concentration on her face as she tried to recall memories of old lore, to look for any sign of hope or good fortune in the tale Séamus had told. Suddenly, her face cleared and she gently pushed Séamus back so that he was at arm's length looking directly at her.

"Now where did you say this man was when you saw him first?" she asked in a gentle, coaxing voice.

"Just outside the front door a bit, over by the garden wall at the front of the house."

"Was he on your right or on your left?"

"On the right I think, yes on the right," said Séamus thinking hard.

The effect of this statement seemed to be to relieve his grandmother of a burden, like she had heard of the recovery of a dear friend who had been ill. She half smiled, her shoulders dropping and slackening as she continued.

"And the wren?"

"On the way out of the bog, on a tree stump, more or less ahead of me I suppose..." said Séamus trying to recall, relaxing a little himself, recognising the easing of tension in his grandmother.

"But the tree stump was on the right side of the track!" he exclaimed smiling, as this he deemed to be the reason of his grandmother's sudden composure resulting from his previous revelation. He had guessed right, for Granny now sat down and patted her lap with the palms of both hands in a satisfied gesture.

"Well then, he meant you no harm anyhow, if Pooka he was," she said, "For they appear on your left if they mean you harm, so they do."

They both smiled at each other in silence for a moment, both feeling the relief of the final positive outcome to the conversation. Then another quizzical look crossed Granny's face.

"Did he say goodbye, Séamus? The man, when you first met him?"

"No. I don't think so. Not goodbye," said Séamus, racking his memory. "What does that mean?" he asked, the quizzical expression now moving across from his Granny's face to make its home on his own features.

"What does it mean? What does it mean indeed?" mused Granny, still in her chair, looking up to the ceiling for inspiration and chewing on her lip as she tried to remember.

"Pookies never say goodbye to anyone!" laughed Granddad, coming in the door from the hallway, followed by his daughter and granddaughter. He must have heard the tail end of the conversation as he approached the sitting room.

"What's this?" enquired Mrs Moran. "Not more about that old man?"

"Johnny the Pookie!" said Sinéad smiling, making a joke of it. She did this for Séamus's sake, rather than trying to tease him, as some of you may have imagined some sisters would do in such circumstances. Sinéad was not that kind of sister I'm pleased to say.

"He's Johnny the Pookie more like!" said Mrs Moran, indicating Séamus with a look. She was smiling, but half in reproach, as if to say, "that's enough of the matter."

"All nonsense anyway," laughed Granddad again, sitting down in his chair and lighting his pipe. He glanced at his wife, who glanced back at him with the same half smile, no words exchanged.

"Tea and cake?" Granny said, getting to her feet again, once more resuming the relay between the kitchen and the sitting room that characterised the dynamic of the house. Granddad was in his chair and Granny was busy, always busy. With this normality returned, everyone got stuck into his or her cake and the conversation returned to the usual topic of cattle.

Chapter 3

Bad Magic

It was now late in the evening and Mrs Moran closed up the small damper for the fire in the range so that it would just tick over in the night and keep the house warm. It wasn't particularly a cold night, but since it was clear, there was a bit of a chill in the air and she also had a little fire of turf and wood put down in the living room too so everyone felt a bit cosier.

It was nearly bedtime for Séamus and Sinéad anyway, with the weather forecast coming on at the end of the nine o'clock news on RTÉ1, Ireland's main television channel. The night was to remain clear and a little chilly. Tomorrow would be fine also; a good day if you wanted to do a little late spraying said the weatherman.

"I'll certainly do that!" exclaimed Mrs Moran who was a great woman for getting out and doing jobs on the farm whenever the opportunity arose. Some of the fields were not in the best condition still, the land being poorer and rougher in general along the northwest coast of Ireland, prone to long bouts of wind and rain for much of the year. But with a few years' hard work, there were some respectable fields now on the Morans' little farmstead.

Others could also become respectable soon with a bit of effort and persistent spraying. This was needed to deal with the even more persistent rushes, and the blasted *buachaláin*, the ragwort that kept coming back despite Mrs Moran's labours. She would pull the ragwort up by the roots if she had the time and the energy, otherwise she kept up with the spraying when she got a chance – assuming the cattle were not going to be in that particular field for a couple of weeks. Mrs Moran hence announced to her children, with a satisfied smile, her intention to be out spraying tomorrow, before additionally announcing that it would not be long before they were off to the *leaba,* their beds.

Just before Séamus and Sinéad were to begin their protest – opening talks on extra minutes that should be allocated to staying-up-time when on half-term holiday – the fire in the living room, until this moment burning tamely and steadily, suddenly roared up the chimney and flamed as if injected with a jet of paraffin. The noise of it and the abrupt increase of light in the direction of the chimney had all heads turned that way in a trice.

Then, a moment later, they were all turned again; first to look at the light-bulb above their heads that had suddenly dimmed, then to look at the door to the living room behind them that suddenly rattled with the increased draft as the draw of the chimney mounted. It brought back memories of the hurricane they had had on St Stephens Day, the day after Christmas, several years ago – only there was not supposed to be any storms anywhere in the country this evening were there?

The surprise was over in a moment for Mrs Moran. She accepted what her senses told her, not what the weatherman had said (when were they ever right anyhow?) and she sprang into action.

"Séamus – make sure all the windows are closed downstairs. Sinéad – you do upstairs," she ordered calmly but with an authority that gave leave to no challenge. Simultaneously, she had put the fireguard up in the living room, having first disturbed the fuel in the fire with a poker so that it burned less fiercely.

Then she remembered the sick calf. It was down below the house in the farmyard. The farmyard was just at the back of the house, down a slope that conveniently prevented the farmyard from spoiling the view and also stopped the smell of silage from wafting straight into the kitchen. The silage bales were arrayed on the right-hand side of the yard as you walked down into it, with the barn on the left and the cattle pen next to the barn and further down the slope on the left-hand side also.

The pen was thus so positioned that you could not see all of it from the house, because of the barn being in the way and because of the drop down into the yard. As a result, despite the sensor lights being on outside the back door and in the yard, Mrs Moran was not sure if the middle gate, which could be used to separate the cattle, was securely closed in the pen. In this wind, the metal gate if loose could injure the calf, which would otherwise have been the safest of the cattle in the storm. The ones out in the fields were probably sheltering amongst trees and would be in some small danger from falling branches, but that was inevitable and unavoidable.

Mrs Moran headed for the kitchen therefore, shouting to Séamus her intention to check the calf, and then went through to the small utility room. Here the back door to the house was located along with a collection of coats, sticks, hats and wellington boots for work on the farm.

In an instant, she was out in the teeth of the storm, lashed by fierce wind and rain. She struggled to close the back door again, steeling herself for the dash to the barn as loose branches and assorted debris from who knows where blew across the lawn before her eyes. Quickly she was off, over the patio adjacent to the lawn behind the house, a distance of a couple of yards to the small gate that led both to the farm entrance and to the track that went down to the barn. She closed the gate again despite the buffeting she got from the wind; otherwise it might have been taken off its hinges by the gale. The gate was set in a gap in the small stone wall, about three feet high (enough to dissuade cattle from jumping it) that surrounded the garden around the house.

It was just after closing the gate before turning again to head down to the farmyard that she heard the thunder. At least she thought it was thunder, but there was a strange drumming rhythm to the noise. It almost seemed that the thunder was coming not from the sky, but up from the bog road towards the farm as if on a visit. Mrs Moran put this down to the confusion caused by the wind screaming in her ears, but it was fortunate that she decided at this point to look in that direction rather than turning for the farmyard. I dread to think what may have occurred it she had not. For when she squinted her eyes to look through the gloom towards the farm entrance, she saw a huge spectral apparition heading straight towards her that she barely had time to avoid.

Instinctively, Mrs Moran managed to roll herself over the top of the garden wall to the side of the gate and onto the lawn, realising she had no time to waste trying to open the gate. She landed safely out of the way, just in time as the black horse thundered up to the gate on the farmyard side, exactly where she had just been standing. It was to be only a brief respite though.

The horse easily jumped the wall, a massive stallion with steam seeming to emanate from its flanks and its nostrils, and it reared over Mrs Moran who was still trying to regain her feet. She put her hands up to shield herself from the blow of the hooves descending upon her, when she heard a shout and felt a tug on her sleeve. The shout distracted the horse from its aim and the tug pulled her a few inches to the side, back towards the house. The horse came down with a crash and a shudder, a hair's breadth from Mrs Moran.

It was enough. Séamus helped his mother to her feet and speedily they retreated backwards towards the door of the house, facing the horse that had turned as if to attack again. It seemed to stare straight at Séamus and its eyes were red as if on fire. It was a terrifying, demonic sight.

Séamus would have been frozen to the spot had he not been arm in arm with his mother who kept their momentum going towards the house. She was looking down at this point to shield her eyes from the wind and did not see the monstrous eyes of the horse. A second later, they were both in the house and the back door was firmly shut.

The horse made no approach towards the house, but leapt over the wall again and sped down into the farmyard. Sounds of banging and neighing and cattle lowing mingled with the wind from outside, whilst Mrs Moran and Séamus abandoned their coats and boots in the utility room and stumbled into the kitchen. Setanta was there now, baring his teeth and barking as if possessed. It took Séamus and Sinéad quite a while to calm him down.

"Someone's horse is loose – though I don't know who that beast belongs to!" said Mrs Moran, mostly to herself to steady her nerves. "Poor thing must be frightened and have gone wild because of the storm; I'll ring your Granddad to see who it belongs to."

Yet the telephone was not working when she lifted the receiver, and soon the lights were not working either. Séamus and Sinéad brought candles out of the cupboard in the utility room. They had no choice now but to wait for the storm to finish. Mrs Moran had decided it was too dangerous to go out and check the calf with a wild horse outside.

Séamus agreed and he remembered the horse's eyes. That was no horse, he thought. But it was a thought he kept to himself.

*

In the morning, the lights and the phone were working again, and Granddad did not know of anyone who owned a large black horse in the area. Mrs Moran had spoken to her brother and sister as well, but they seemed to be unaware of last night's storm. They thought that the night had been still, just as the weatherman had said it would.

"That's very strange," she said to her children who had been waiting for her to finish her calls, "everyone else seems to have slept through that storm. Must have been a freak local thing I suppose. We'll have to go and check the damage now anyhow. I hope that berserk horse didn't clatter into too much down in the yard."

That hope was unfortunately a forlorn one. The damage was worse than Mrs Moran or anyone else could have possibly imagined. The first things that Séamus noticed were the blackberry bushes near the farm entrance. What berries had remained were turned to mush, not as if battered by rain or wind, but as if the plants had been suffering from some sort of blight. Later that morning when he had looked at other bushes that he knew of located around their fields, they all seemed to have suffered the same fate. Not a berry remained on Dooleen Hill Farm.

Mrs Moran was not concerned about the blackberries however. It was the sight of the silage bales that bothered her. Not one was untouched. Some were actually pushed upright (they had all been lying horizontally) and all bore signs of a frenzied assault, the black lining ripped and shredded. Hoof and teeth marks were evident on all. The children gaped and Mrs Moran stood in stunned silence. She would never be able to repair all of the bales with tape; the rips and holes were too big. The air would get at the silage and it would be ruined. They would have no fodder for the animals in winter.

And if this was not bad enough, sadly, it was not to be the final blow. After what seemed an age taking in the scene and assessing the damage done to the bales, Mrs Moran and the children walked down together to the pen. Nobody said a word, expecting the worst. The calf lay unmoving before them; the briefest look confirmed that it had died, although there were no marks upon it to suggest an attack by the horse.

Séamus thought it must have died of fright.

Chapter 4

A Pookie in the Barn

Granny and Granddad arrived in the afternoon. They were moving cattle up from Kilagan to Dooleen as some of the fields in the village adjacent to Dooleen Hill Farm belonged to Mrs Moran's parents. They also wanted to hear the story of last night's goings-on for themselves of course.

Mrs Moran had made a pot of tea and they sat around the range in the kitchen discussing the matter.

"Sure it was bound to happen," muttered Granny to herself, looking down at her hands and rolling her thumbs.

"What was? What do you mean?" asked Mrs Moran perplexed.

"Oh, don't heed her – just superstitions," said Granddad flicking a look at his wife. "Séamus," he continued, "go and get me the silage fork from the barn will you – I want to see what state it is in. I'll see later what we can do about saving some of that fodder."

Séamus went off as he was bidden. He couldn't help feeling that the adults wanted him out of the way so they could discuss things amongst themselves. Sinéad had already taken herself away to watch some television, not wanting to hear the same story again or details of assorted cattle. But Séamus, who had seen the red eyes of the horse, had wanted a chance to discuss it with Granny.

What could be wrong with the silage fork anyway he mused, as he opened the door to the smallest part of the barn where the tools were kept. Setanta had run out with him and then went sniffing around to the central part of the barn where the hay and turf were stacked.

Séamus returned to the house and handed the silage fork to his Granddad. This was longer than an ordinary garden fork that you might be more used to, also having longer thinner, curved prongs attached to the end.

"That looks grand, thanks," said Granddad, looking at Séamus with a smile.

"No problem," said Séamus, turning and heading for the door again hearing Setanta barking.

"I'll just go and see what Setanta is up to," he added.

It was obvious that he was as well off outside running around with his dog as the conversation had gone quiet again as soon as he had re-entered the kitchen.

Séamus ran down towards the barn and entered the wide middle section, dodging around the old Massey Ferguson tractor that was parked outside. Setanta had ceased his barking now, but Séamus was sure that this was where he had heard it. Maybe there was a rat up in the loft and Setanta had somehow got up there, scrambling over the stacked turf.

Thinking this, Séamus entered looking upwards and to the right where the ladder rested. At first he did not see the unusual shape in the shadows, on the left of that section of the barn, but his eyes soon registered the figure that was out of place and he turned to see the same strange old man that he had spoken to, two days before.

The old man walked out of the shadow towards Séamus. Séamus felt uneasy at the look in the man's eye as he squinted at him, and the thought ran in his mind that Granny had been pleased the last time when he said the old man had appeared on the right-hand side of him. This time, he was undoubtedly on his left.

"You shouldn't turn your back on a stranger in trouble," the man said, taking another step towards Séamus.

"What? I didn't—" began Séamus.

"The old laws of hospitality have been broken. Now what would be a fitting punishment do you think?" interrupted the man. As he spoke he stepped nearer again.

Séamus, at first, felt as you or I would feel if we were wrongly or mistakenly accused of something. He was upset and annoyed, frustrated by the misunderstanding but unable to account for it. However, the main feeling that came over him after that was one of fear; fear of this strange old man, his unfriendly bearing and his sinister words.

Séamus started to back up out of the barn, once more trying to protest that he had done the man no harm. But the words came out in a low inaudible kind of a stutter, which failed to even convince him.

"N-no... I haven't... I d-did...I mean," he stammered.

"And where do you think you are going?" asked the old man, straightening up for the first time and taking on an even greater menace.

Then many things seemed to happen all at once. Bits of wood and turf and buckets left in the barn started flying up and around Séamus as if he were the centre of a small whirlwind. The sound of Setanta barking loudly assailed Séamus from somewhere above him. And the old man was changing.

Séamus raised his arms to protect himself and spun about confused, now retreating back into the barn. Then, before his very eyes, Séamus saw a creature that he could only associate with fairy stories of his earlier childhood.

An ugly, mostly bald, lumpy green head with small evil looking eyes and a mouth full of vicious teeth faced Séamus above a dirty white smock. This adorned a thick, muscular body with uncovered, long sinewy limbs. The creature stood over six feet tall, despite being hunched, and Séamus correctly identified it as a troll, a hideous troll to be precise.

"Yes, a fitting punishment!" sneered the troll. "Let's see – I can grind his bones to make some bread," it said advancing on Séamus. "No, no, that's a giant, won't do at all. I know – I'll turn you into a toad! No, that's a witch isn't it?"

Séamus retreated back into the end of the barn where the turf was stacked, the troll now between him and the entrance since the confusion of the whirlwind. It was now that he saw Setanta above him still barking madly. Or rather, it was Setanta's head.

The dog's head hovered between himself and the troll, bearing its teeth at the latter, eight or nine feet off the ground. Unfortunately, Setanta's head seemed unable to adjust its height or position and could only move around, snapping at the air in impotent fury whilst the sneering troll advanced again on the cornered Séamus.

Now you must remember that Séamus was only twelve, so despite his rage at seeing his dog in such a plight, the unexpected and frightening sight of the advancing troll paralysed him and he could neither move nor speak. Part of him wanted to run and attack the troll that had done this terrible thing to his beloved pet, another part told him to try and run past the creature and get to safety. The conflicting emotions only served to keep him stock-still and tense where he stood, his fists and indeed all his body clenched like a compressed spring ready to explode, in any and all directions. Something in this posture of Séamus seemed to trouble the troll momentarily and it stopped to appraise its prey.

Then the sneer reappeared and the troll returned to its theme, taking another step nearer. "Ah yes, I'm a troll. I know," it said, raising its arms above its head and stretching its fingers out to reveal cruel claws, "I'll gobble him up!"

Setanta was now frantic in his barking, his head spinning around on the spot in the air; as Séamus crouched down to try to parry the oncoming assault. Then, suddenly, an unexpected voice came from the entrance to the barn shouting, "You'll do no such thing!"

Séamus looked up and the troll spun around. Granddad stood there with the silage fork held out in front of him, pointed purposefully at the troll.

The troll laughed then, rocking his head backwards and holding his stomach in a mocking gesture.

"Do you think you can do me any harm with that?" he roared, slapping his thighs in delight.

"Take a closer look," said Granddad quietly, moving into the barn closer to the troll.

Now the monster was in a position where it could not move out of the barn without running the gauntlet of Granddad and his silage fork.

A strange new expression of amazement mixed with fear rested on the troll's ugly features as it noticed, tied with baling twine (you should always carry some of this in your pocket for it has a thousand uses), a sprig of holly and a sprig of mistletoe were attached to the outer prongs of the fork.

"Yes, that's right," smiled Granddad. "You can't use any magic around me now and this will skewer you quite nicely, sir."

The troll wiped the back of his left hand across its slavering jaws and puffed its chest out, stating with another sneer, "You seem very confident of your lore, old fool. Why don't you and the brat clear off now whilst I hold my temper – your bravery deserves that much I'll grant you."

Séamus nodded his head vigorously at this. Granddad had done enough to unsettle the troll, but it was best not to push it. He desperately wanted to be the other side of the thing and did not stop to consider any more than that.

"Nothing doing, Pooka!" answered Granddad though, to Séamus's dismay. "I'm confident alright, and you are too, else you'd have made a move by now. You will put all the things right that you've put wrong with your bad magic. You will swear on your life not to harm anyone in my family – including our animals – again. And then you'll vanish and go. Agree to this now before I get to three or you'll sleep quiet in a barrow until the end of time."

And having dictated his terms, Granddad now advanced steadily on the troll, counting as he came, "*A haon, A do, A tri…*"

Séamus held his breath, whilst the troll retreated a step back towards him with each step forward of his grandfather's.

"Okay! Okay!" yelled the troll at last, raising its hands in the air like a soldier surrendering. Granddad had just come to "*A trí*", pulling the fork back as if ready to thrust.

Its head sank on its chest and it sighed heavily. Under its breath in a sad voice, it said, "I'll do as you say."

"*An mhaith*," said Granddad, meaning very good, exhaling heavily himself. Séamus could see the sweat on his brow and the look of concern etched on his face. How confident had his grandfather really been of success he wondered?

Granddad lowered the silage fork, placing the prongs so that they touched the ground. At this, the troll retook the form of the strange old man and, after taking a moment to compose himself, he mumbled a series of commands into his chest, making small hand movements close to his face.

"It is finished," he said. "All has been undone. All that could be. You have my word. And no harm will come to you or your family or anything belonging to your family, by me or on my behest. You have my word on that also. Are you satisfied?" He looked defiantly again at Granddad, speaking once more with some of the original haughty pride that he had shown before Granddad's timely interruption.

"Yes. Satisfied, thank you," said Granddad, bowing slightly, with a respectful air that puzzled Séamus all the more.

With a nod of satisfaction, the strange old man touched his hat and returned the bow. Then he was gone, disappearing into thin air as if he had never been.

Setanta, thankfully intact once more and back on terra firma, leaped up and licked Séamus's hands. Séamus hugged him with delight.

"You okay?" asked Granddad.

"Yes. Yes, thank you," replied Séamus through a huge grin of relief and joy at Setanta's return.

Granddad left the fork down then and turned to go back to the house.

"Put this back then, there's a great man," he said, and turning, muttered under his breath, "All a load of nonsense."

Chapter 5

What Johnny had to say

It was bad enough for Mrs Moran to see all the bales back in place and repaired as if nothing had happened. Granddad's explanation that they weren't that bad after all and it only took a bit of graft and a bit of tape was simply incredulous. And if Mrs Moran had then examined the bales closer and found they were as good as before, with no signs of any tape being put on them to repair the tears, she would have thought an elaborate trick had been played on her and would have got very angry indeed. Already Sinéad and Séamus had slipped quietly into Sinéad's room to talk and hide from the potential fallout of such an occurrence. But the calf changed everything.

When Granddad asked, "Did you examine that animal in the pen very closely?" Mrs Moran was distracted from the subject of the bales. She cared far more for the well being of her livestock than about damaged or repaired fodder, and she rounded on Granddad as if he had accused her.

"There were no marks on him, he didn't survive that freak storm that's all. I did everything I could!" she said, trying not to raise her voice.

"That's not what I meant," said Granddad with a smile. "I know you did a good job on the calf; I saw him back on his feet a moment ago when I fetched Séamus from the barn."

Mrs Moran stood with her mouth hanging open. She hadn't actually gone and touched the calf or examined him up close. From a couple of yards away he had obviously been dead. The other damage in the farmyard had been too much for her on top of that and she had returned to the kitchen for a strong cup of tea to steady her nerves. Could it really be that he wasn't dead after all? He had been so still though.

Without another word she headed out of the house and down to the pen. The calf was standing there and looked well enough to be let out again with the other cattle. She had indeed done a good job, the poor thing must have got a knock on the head or something like that in the storm and had looked dead, but there was no evidence of any injury to be concerned about. "Well," she said to herself, "I'll not pronounce judgment on an animal again until I've checked it for a pulse!"

Happily she went back up to the house. She would have to call the vet again to cancel his visit to examine the animal and register the cause of death. How embarrassing, she thought, to have to say that the calf was not dead after all. But she didn't really care about that.

No more was said after that about the mysteriously repaired bales or the storm or the incidents of that strange night. Mrs Moran was reconciled with the calf's survival and did not feel the need to understand what obviously could not be adequately explained. Her mother and father were quite clearly satisfied with the outcome of events, so she contented herself with that. It was a good job that she had not noticed the withered blackberries though, for seeing them restored to their former ripe condition would have been perhaps one mystery too many.

Séamus noticed, but kept the information to himself. They wouldn't be around much longer now anyway, certainly not the ones close to the house where Sinéad and himself would soon finish them off. It had been quite a day already and he stayed indoors mostly that afternoon which was unusual for him. He did go outside two or three times though just to pet Setanta and to reassure himself the dog's head was the right way around.

The next morning was more like a November day in the West of Ireland. Rain and more rain. There was not a chance of spraying the rushes now, the rain would dilute the formula and make it ineffective. Mrs Moran wondered if she would get any more chances this year at all.

Every now and then there was a break or a lightening in the strength of the downpour so that one or other of the household could go down to the barn to get more fuel for the range, or go out to check the cattle. Once a day would normally suffice for ensuring the cattle were okay, but Mrs Moran wanted a close eye kept on the calf that had been sick. So Séamus was sent to have another look at them in the afternoon, Mrs Moran having seen them herself in the morning and having been quite happy with their condition. Séamus was content to do this, and he soon had his old coat and hat on, the ones used for mucky farm duties, followed by his wellingtons. Then he grabbed a good sturdy stick.

The land would be very wet at this time of year and a stick could be very useful if you got yourself suddenly stuck in mud, or if you needed to fend off a cow that got over excited thinking you might be bringing it some dairy nuts. Strange how their usual fear of humans disappeared if they thought you had food for them. Fortunately for Séamus, the cattle were only two fields away in what they called the Round Field, and they could be checked without having to go through any of the wetter, boggier land where you could struggle to get a firm footing. They all seemed content and well. A few were lying down so Séamus walked towards them shouting "Up!" and he tapped a couple that didn't take the hint with his stick. He did this so he could check them properly and see that none were limping, marked, or in any way under the weather.

Pleased with what he saw, Séamus went to a rocky outcrop in the middle of the Round Field to sit down and have a think. It was one of his favourite places. The field dipped down towards one of the Dooleen lakes, so you could sit the other side of the small collection of large rocks and vegetation in the middle of the field, out of view of the house and looking over the lake. A rowan tree and an ash tree stood either side of the feature like goalposts, about six metres apart, with mostly blackberry bushes in between covering the rocks. It was a quiet, peaceful, timeless place, and you felt as if you could belong to any age when you were there.

He had no idea what this outcrop used to be, if anything other than an area where rocks were dumped when the field was cleared. But he had often fancied in his imagination that it was the remains of an old dwelling, or perhaps a barrow where someone important, maybe a Celtic Chief, had been laid to rest.

Whilst thinking of this, a movement to his right caught his eye, and Séamus turned his head to see what it was. Sitting, facing him, was once again the strange old man in his gaudy clothes.

"I used to live here once," he said.

Séamus leapt to his feet facing the old man. "You promised you wouldn't bother us again!"

The old man stayed sitting serenely and smiled at Séamus. "I said I would do you no harm, and I won't. I still need your help though."

"Why should I help you now!" spat Séamus indignantly. "After all you did – it wasn't my fault, I didn't know what you were after, you hardly gave me a chance, and then..."

Séamus trailed off, realising he was losing the run of himself in his anger, as he saw the old man motioning with his palms up appealing for calm.

"Quite right, quite right," the old man said. "After all these years you'd think I'd have learned a little patience and a cooler temper. But I'm out of sorts and out of my place so to speak, and it weighs heavy on me Séamus, so it does. It weighs heavy."

The old man seemed to be looking through Séamus, conjuring up memories in his mind, a fatigued and empty look in his eyes. There was a profound sadness and sense of loss as he spoke and Séamus felt it.

Against his better judgement, almost compelled, he joked, smiling nervously, "Okay, let's hear it, Johnny the Pookie".

The old man focused directly on Séamus now, and laughed.

"Johnny the Pookie eh?" he said. "Yes, that fits. That fits. Well here is my story, as I choose to tell it, and you'll know yourself by the end of it what it is I hope for, and what part I ask you to play."

Séamus sat down to listen and the old man leant on his stick, closed his eyes, like a *sennachai* (a Celtic storyteller of old), and recited his tale in a mesmerising, almost musical tone.

"Once there were many paths between our world and yours, and others besides. The land of youth some called our home because we aged not. *Tír na nÓg*, the Otherworld. We were revered as gods, with powers in this world that seemed like magic, some of us gifted with fearsome strength and uncanny abilities. Our people became known as the *Tuatha De Danaan,* the people of the Goddess Danu. No doubt you recognise that name from stories or myths that you have been told. Other creatures came from our world also, some destructive or with no peaceful intent, and we protected men of this world from them, fought with them and eventually defeated them. Balor was their king. In those days, some of your people came to our world also and they found that they had powers there that we did not, and they lived a long time in youth and happiness.

"But times changed. The paths became less used and our powers here seemed to lessen. Other people then came to Ireland, and other shores where we held sway, the Milesians you may have heard of, the Celts. They challenged our supremacy and their Druids were both powerful and knowledgeable so that we were forced to make way for them. The people of this land now made their own destiny, forged their own kingdoms. Most of the *Tuatha De Danaan* remained, some on islands off the Western shore, others building magical palaces underground, mixing still in the affairs of this world, unable to accept their diminished role. These mounds were known as the *Sidhe*, as later their inhabitants became known, places where mortals would go, or be taken, and share in the eternal youth of their hosts. But this interference was mostly unwelcome; the mounds were often attacked, dug up and laid waste by Druids and warriors. Soon hardly any of our halls remained.

"Then the people also embraced a new faith, a new truth. They worshipped the One God and had no need for our counsels at all, no desire to worship the former powers. This, of course, was how it should be. Our time had come; it was the natural order of things. Most that had remained deserted their mounds now, yet many, after so long in this world, could still not find it in their hearts to leave. They remained, as did their retainers, for good or for evil. But their power and influence lessened the more. It was not long in our reckoning before those that stayed were diminished beings, merely feared, and then worse, ignored. Many fought this indignation bitterly, some turning bad and creating mischief, others using the powers that remained to them to achieve good or to just keep themselves secret, using means that people saw merely as magic. This mostly created more fear, sometimes changing the destiny of men for worse, not better. Many, as a result, now chose to sleep and were lost to all worlds. Those that had the will to go on, if they still had the power and remembered the paths, now returned to the Otherworld – some with black hearts, stealing children away with them in a last bitter revenge on the world that had turned its back upon them. Those that did not sleep, but now lacked the power or the knowledge to go home, led a solitary life ignoring the world as it ignored them. Sometimes they meddled for good – as most were good-natured – others sometimes would cause trouble where they felt slighted by those who roamed where they had once ruled. We became known as Pooka, Fearshee or Banshee, Fairies and countless other names. Our servants that remained were lesser beings still, being remembered by name only as those who had served Lugh, *Lugh Chorpain*, Leprechauns, living meaningless existences on their own, hoarding parts of their masters' former treasures. Once mighty rulers, revered as gods, we are now remembered as little more than mere imps and pranksters."

Johnny paused at this point as if to contemplate all that he had said. Séamus didn't move a muscle, spellbound by what he had heard spoken and chanted, seeing in his mind's eye all that had befallen over numerous centuries. Then Johnny continued and got to the point.

"Ah me! I have the knowledge and no little power left to me, ahem, as you have seen. But I have long since known that I needed another to make the crossing – one from this world to assist me. You, Séamus, I see that you are to be the one. You can end my exile and help to send me home."

Johnny stopped his tale, and it was as if a switch had been turned off. Séamus snapped out of his reverie and a thousand thoughts and questions crowded his brain. All he managed for the moment though was, "Why me?"

"I have an instinct, Séamus, trust me, you have the power in you to help me. And I do not know why you – why anyone? The real question is; will you help?"

Séamus's head was spinning. "But how will I get back from the Otherworld if I help you cross over. And what if it all goes wrong – what will happen to us then?"

"If it goes wrong, it simply won't work. We will not go anywhere. You and I will not be harmed, although it is perhaps my last chance. I am weary, and if you cannot get me home I think it will be time for me to find a barrow of my own and sleep until the next age comes."

Johnny paused in thought for a moment again, as if the implications of what he had said were as new to him as they were to Séamus.

"But I feel it will work," he continued, enthusiastic once more, "and once a path has been reopened, you will have no difficulty going back – the one time anyway. I can show you how and I have promised, have I not, that I will not harm you?"

Johnny spoke evenly and with a controlled dignity, although Séamus could sense the excitement in the old man, the Pookie, whatever he was. There was an ancient pride in his bearing that Séamus did not want to offend. He felt that the old man had been honest, laid bare his hopes, his fears, and that he, Séamus, must decide now one way or the other. And whatever he decided would be final, he was sure that he would not be asked again.

Looking back, Séamus could not have said what it was that made him say what he said at that moment. It made no sense; it was ridiculous, yet it was as if there was really no other choice. To refuse would have meant an endless regret for an adventure passed by and a lost soul left unaided.

"I'll help so," was simply all that he said.

Johnny the Pookie smiled.

Chapter 6

The Reek

The two conspirators sat for a long time in the Round Field talking about the undertaking that they had just agreed to. Sometimes Séamus had to get Johnny to repeat what he was saying as he talked so quickly and with such enthusiasm about what they should do now.

It transpired that the path to the Otherworld that Johnny knew, and thought he could open with the help of Séamus, was on top of a mountain that Séamus knew very well.

Johnny said it was on the mountain you could see from the front of Séamus's house, only a few miles away, the Holy mountain of Croagh Patrick. A church had been built on top of the mountain where St Patrick was said to have banished all serpents from Ireland.

Every year on the last Sunday of July was Reek Sunday. Thousands of pilgrims would climb the Reek on that day and hear Mass at the top of the mountain from the little church. Of course, before the coming of the One God and the time of St Patrick, it had still been an important and revered holy place for the people of Ireland, and of the province of Connaught in particular, Johnny told Séamus. And on the summit, he said, near where the church now stood, was an entrance, one that could only be opened by those who knew how. A gateway to the Otherworld.

"Well, no time like the present," he announced finally, getting up and stretching with a purposeful air.

"What do you mean? We can't go now," complained Séamus. "You can probably whisk yourself off there by some magic, but I'll need a lift – it's a good ten miles by road –

and I'll also need a very good excuse for climbing the Reek at this time of year!"

Johnny creased up his face and paced backwards and forwards, trying to contain his temper. "Well, what do you suggest? You're not changing your mind on me already are you, Séamus?" he said, flapping his arms, a distressed note in his voice.

"Calm down," said Séamus softly, trying to sound calm himself. Johnny had promised not to harm him, but how binding was that promise he wondered, and could the Pookie control its temper if faced with another disappointment? Séamus was committed to helping now anyway, and he wanted to help. He wanted to get a glimpse of the Otherworld, the land that had inspired so many legends.

"Granddad goes to town, Westport that is, on Fridays, and sometimes further, to the Tavern at Murrisk," he said, pacing himself now and thinking up a plan as he talked to Johnny. "He meets with other farmers in some sort of political gathering of Fine Gael supporters I think. I could ask to go with him – I often do – and meet up with him a few hours later as usual. If he goes to Westport, I can try and hitch a ride from there to Murrisk, or even get a taxi on Bridge Street. But if he goes to the Tavern; well I'm practically there – it's only a short walk to the car park where the climb begins."

Séamus was getting excited himself now, smiling at his plan and how it all fitted together. He could get away tomorrow and head up the Reek and nobody would know his business.

"I'll phone him this evening, see if I can turn it so that he suggests the Tavern to the others, if they haven't picked another place already. Then, my friend, we are in business!"

Johnny jumped up at this and placed both hands over Séamus's. He began swinging him around in a dance, lifting his feet high off the ground as he jigged. If anyone had seen him, they would have marvelled at the activity and strength of such an old man. As it was, Séamus was the only witness, and he was now so completely caught up with the adventure that he shared in his new comrade's delight and jigged around with him. It was as if he himself were heading home at last after centuries in foreign lands.

It turned out even better than expected. Most recent meetings had been in Westport itself, at the Market Bar. So, in fairness to those out beyond the quays, the Tavern in Murrisk had already been selected as tomorrow's venue for West Mayo's Fine Gael Farmers to once again put the world to rights.

Granddad was always happy to have Séamus for company and was content with the explanation that he wanted to go on the drive and then get some fresh air walking up towards and around the base of the Reek.

"Mind when you get there; no further than the gate after the statue," said Granddad on the phone. "Remember it's November and no time for going up the Reek, especially on your own."

Séamus felt a little guilty agreeing to this, he hated deceiving the people that he loved, but it was necessary. It is always a bit easier lying to someone on a telephone though, as they cannot see your face and read the lie in your eyes.

The next morning therefore, around eleven o'clock, Séamus headed off for his grandparents' house. He declined a lift from his mother, wanting to stretch his legs to warm up for the long climb ahead by walking the couple of miles to Kilagan.

He had some cheese sandwiches in a cellophane wrapper in one pocket of his coat, and a small bottle of water in another, anticipating that he would want something to eat, probably when he was halfway up the mountain. Nobody had seen his preparations and nobody would question him taking a stick from the back of the house for his walk, either to his grandparents or about the base of Croagh Patrick. You should always have a good stick if you are walking on uneven ground, moving cattle, or especially if you are climbing or descending a mountain.

Sinéad was playing with Setanta outside the back door when he left the house. She stopped what she was doing however and, after Séamus said goodbye to her, she replied, "*Slán*, Séamus. Be careful at the Reek."

This may have been an innocent enough thing to say, but there was something in her tone, a hint of worry and sadness that made Séamus stop and look at his sister. He wondered for a moment if she knew.

He sometimes called her 'The Witch' in jest, as she often seemed to know things he had thought secret or she would know what he was thinking. He couldn't meet her eyes as he answered, "*Slán*, Sinéad. I will," and he turned to go.

"Just a minute," said his sister, jogging up to his side, and she slipped a small metal object into one of his hands. Séamus looked at it. It was one of Sinéad's brooches that she sometimes wore. She had always liked jewellery and Granny had given her this when she was very young.

"I know it's silly, but you should take this," she said quickly. "I find it very uncomfortable walking along in the rain this time of year. You need the top button undone on your blouse for your breathing, but there is such a gap to the next button and you end up cold and wet and with a sore throat the next day. So I just clip this below the button and it steadies the ship, so to speak, with only half the gap between the first two buttons open instead of the whole thing. They always put the buttons too far apart."

Séamus just looked at her a little nonplussed at the gift and the explanation. There was perhaps a modicum of sense in it, but not much really. Sensing his doubt, Sinéad added more softly. "It looks like it will be a windy day. And it's a lucky charm. Granny got it from her grandmother. It's very old."

Séamus nodded. He felt strangely warm and touched by his sister's concern for him, almost tearful. He put the brooch onto his shirt beneath his coat, a light waterproof, between the first two buttons as she had suggested.

"Thank you," was all he could say. Sinéad grinned broadly at him.

"Have a good day!" she said, all the previous gravity suddenly leaving her, and she skipped off across the lawn with Setanta at her heels.

Séamus finally headed down the Dooleen road away from the house. He looked down, trying to see the brooch again without taking it off, concerned that it might look a bit 'girly', in which case, off it would come as soon as he was out of sight of home. But it was a plain enough, functional brooch, just a circle really, too tarnished to make out exactly what pattern was on it, although Séamus fancied he could see some sort of a face in one part of it. He shrugged and zipped up his waterproof a little more as the predictable rain began. You couldn't see the brooch now anyhow, and Sinéad was probably in one of her 'be weirdly over-nice' moods. There was no way she could have known of his plans, the gift was just a whim.

It was not long after half past eleven when Séamus arrived at his grandparents' house. Unusually, Granddad was nearly ready to go and they soon headed off in his old Ford Cortina which, more unusually, started first time.

It was a short drive, first over to Westport, then out through the quays and finally down to Murrisk and the Tavern. A pleasant little drive of half an hour, at Granddad's steady pace. It was getting on for half past twelve and the evidence in the car park indicated that a few of the other farmers had arrived. There were other old cars, some fairly battered, and a few tractors, most even older than the cars. Some car boots and tractor doors were held in place only by baling twine and some car aerials had been fastened out of miscellaneous pieces of wire or bent-up old coat hangers.

Séamus entered the Tavern with his Granddad and politely said hello to some of the people he knew before they had their lunch and before he headed off on his planned climb. They were in more or less the same state as their vehicles. All old, some very smart and in good nick, but some very battered with bits of clothing held together by assorted ingenious methods, baling twine included of course. Most had caps on their heads and were loath to remove them; even now they were inside the warmer climes of the public bar.

Séamus could hear his mother in his head saying something about a 'Chamber of Horrors' under her breath and he couldn't help but smile. They all seemed to have nicknames as well, and would refer to each other by them when speaking together about an absent friend, but only when the owner of the title was not about. They would politely use each other's real names in such a large gathering here today though, and Séamus wondered if any of them knew what they were called when they were not around. His grandfather was for some reason referred to as 'The Lone Ranger', and Séamus recognised 'The Badger', 'Porridge Face', 'How are ye all', 'The Snake' and 'Tablets' in the bar. He was not sure who all the others were, but did not doubt that they laid claim to similar bizarre titles. 'The Sheriff', 'The Deputy' and 'The Gangster' were not here yet. 'Nervous Eddie' was just coming in the door with 'Turbot' and 'The Weanling'.

Séamus said goodbye to his grandfather, promising to be back by four thirty and not to climb too high beyond the statue of St Patrick at the base of the Reek, no further than the gate.

"Take care, Séamus. Don't lose yourself!" said Granddad as Séamus departed. Again, Séamus would normally have ignored such a comment, but with the day that was in it, it set him thinking again about how secure his secret was. It was of small matter now though. Séamus was committed to his adventure and on his way. He walked the small distance to the car park at the base of the mountain, opposite the Famine

Memorial, looking out to Clew Bay and practically at sea level. He crossed the car park and then he began to climb the Reek.

The statue of St Patrick was barely beyond the car park, up a number of steep steps, and then there was a short climb to a fence with a gate after that before the real climb began. Granddad knew that Séamus could not reasonably be expected to go no further up than the gate, but it was a good marker to use to set the limits.

Séamus knew that to walk to the Reek from The Tavern, climb it, do whatever they had to do at the top and then descend again was going to take more than four hours. He hoped to get it done in less than six though, and there was no way Granddad and his friends would really be finished at half four. Most of them would need a taxi or a lift home and would not be going until seven or later, having had their fill of porter and whiskey.

Thinking about all of this Séamus almost forgot he was still on his own as he began his ascent and arrived at the statue. Here he stopped for a quick look back out across Clew Bay and its many islands – said to be one for each day of the year – when he was suddenly aware of another presence. He turned again and there was Johnny smiling broadly at him, keen and ready for the off. A livelier looking old man you would not have seen.

"I wondered when you would turn up," laughed Séamus, glad of the company at last. "I'm a bit tight for time, you couldn't magic us up to the top could you?"

"Sorry, Séamus my lad," said Johnny. "There are some things I can do, moving objects a small bit, changing the nature of things, transporting myself where my eye alights, and many an illusion. But levitating you that far – I'm afraid that is beyond my abilities."

Then, after a thought, he added, "I could turn you into a dog for the climb – you'd get up easier and faster on four legs. You might feel a bit funny for a few days after I turn you back, but if you really need to save the time…"

"I'll go as I am thanks!" said Séamus quickly, not sure how serious Johnny was, but in no way wanting to put him to the test.

Without another word, the two of them now began their long climb. Johnny's movements seemed effortless and Séamus imagined that he was just keeping him company and that he could fly up the Reek or appear at the summit if he wished. Séamus on the other hand, despite having climbed the mountain a couple of times before, was hard pushed on the steep slopes. The wind was picking up and with the rain getting heavier the ground was getting more slippery underfoot. It was no day to be climbing, as the warning sign at the base of the mountain had made very clear. Nevertheless, there is almost always someone climbing Croagh Patrick and Séamus could pick out a few shapes further up, all seemingly heading down.

Johnny had produced some magic to keep the rain and wind off them so they seemed to walk in a kind of sheltered bubble. This had to be abandoned however whenever someone coming down walked past them. Some of the hill walkers passed comment on the conditions at the top. It was very cold and windy they said, but you were above the worst clouds and got some good views of the bay in between the passing of the higher clouds, if you were patient enough for them to clear. Séamus nodded his head at the information, but noticed that he and Johnny were the only people going up now and that the weather was worsening. There would probably be no view at all by the time they reached the top, not that that was why he was climbing on this occasion.

There is not much more to say about that climb. Because Séamus was quite fit and had climbed the Reek before, he managed to get to the summit in a little less than two hours despite the conditions. The first part got steadily steeper but then flattened out so that there was an easier middle section where you could catch your breath and recover a little. You turn to your right and walk towards the third, final part of the climb, over relatively easy, slightly undulating ground. The final part is the steepest of all but not the longest, although it feels like it. You walk on sliding shale. It is tough, slippery ground and you struggle to ascend and keep your feet at the same time. The sight of the church as you finally reach the top lifts the spirits though and the strains of the climb are soon forgotten.

As Johnny and Séamus reached the summit, the weather had unexpectedly cleared and they had breathtaking views around Clew Bay and to the Sheefry Hills to the South. Clare Island looked magnificent and beautiful and Séamus could imagine the Pirate Queen, Granuaile, who had a stronghold there in the sixteenth century, looking out defiantly at the seas.

He retreated from the edge and turned his back on the views very quickly however. The wind that high up was icy cold. Séamus was soon huddled against the side of the church for shelter finishing off his sandwiches, half of which he had already eaten on his way up. Johnny stood nearby, patiently waiting for Séamus to be ready and to recover some strength.

At last Séamus turned to him and asked, "What happens now?"

"We prepare ourselves. Here, we'll both hold my staff and concentrate. Rest your stick under your arm there. Now, I will think about my land, the time and place when I left. You just focus your thoughts on helping me to get home, opening the path to my world."

Séamus wasn't sure about the instructions and what exactly he should think of, but he did as Johnny said. He tried to imagine himself and Johnny stepping out on a road that led to Johnny's home. Johnny seemed to be concentrating hard as well, his face screwed up and his lips mumbling in hope and fear, urging the gateway to his world to appear.

Séamus felt a tingle, like a surge of power in his hands, and the temperature dropped further. A mist had begun to form on the top of the mountain so that all views were obscured, but thankfully there was still no rain to accompany it. In seconds, Séamus could barely see the church next to them, all he could see was Johnny beside him and even he was not clear. The effort of concentration was becoming over burdensome, and the strange tingle of power like static electricity, spreading all over his arms, seemed to drain him of strength.

At last he panted desperately to Johnny, "I need a break. I can't see any path. I don't think this is working."

"Not working?" replied Johnny, in a strangely different voice, younger and deeper than before. "There are many types of path, Séamus. It has worked; Séamus, you have given me the strength to get home."

And with that, Johnny stepped away from Séamus, taking his staff with him, disappearing into the mist. Séamus collapsed, sitting down where he had stood, not questioning what he had been told. He was just relieved that the mental exertion that seemed to have drained him so physically was finally at an end.

"Goodbye, Johnny!" he shouted into the mist, closing his eyes and breathing deeply. "I'll not come with you – I wanted to and I know you said I could get back easy enough, but I think it's best I stayed here after all. All the best!"

He opened his eyes again and moved to get back on his feet with the aid of his stick. The mist was clearing fast and in seconds it was gone.

Séamus stood spellbound by the sudden change, the temperature rising as the mist cleared and the surrounding country became visible again to his eyes. The shape of a man sat stooped, twenty yards away with his back to Séamus, but this only caught his attention for an instant; there were far more important things to take note of.

He was on top of a mountain, the size and shape of the Reek that he knew. But around him now were other hills and mountains, Croagh Patrick was no longer an isolated pinnacle, no longer the famous landmark that he knew. Flabbergasted, Séamus then noticed that the church was no longer there, the ground under his feet being far grassier than the bare top of the mountain he had been standing on a moment ago.

And Clew Bay was gone. Below the summit were small rolling hills, fields and signs of little villages dotted about here and there. One hill away to the West bore an uncanny resemblance to the shape of Clare Island, but Granuaile would be sailing nowhere from there. The sea itself was barely visible, far away to the North West, perhaps around where Achill Island should have been.

The realisation hit him at this moment. He had not moved. He was in the same place but, at the same time, in a different place.

Séamus was in the Otherworld.

Chapter 7

Séamus in The Otherworld

The man nearby had got to his feet. The figure that approached him was a match for the new and different voice that Séamus had heard earlier. He was a young, strong-limbed man, no more than thirty years of age. But the grin was unmistakable. Séamus comprehended at once that it was Johnny the Pookie who was walking towards him.

Johnny was dressed in brightly coloured yellow patterned trews accompanied by a red cloak, with a sword suspended around his waist. He lifted Séamus to his feet. Séamus had collapsed and had been sitting down in a lump in the grass. The sudden change in geography following the exertion to get Johnny home had sapped the last of his energy.

Once back on his feet though, Séamus took a moment to review his own appearance. To his surprise, but no longer to his amazement considering all else that had occurred, he found that his garb was similarly altered to a rather more historic style. He was now wearing dark trews, thankfully duller than Johnny's, with boots laced up to his knees the same as his companion, and a dark green cloak pinned with a brooch. The brooch was the same at least, the one he had been given by Sinéad. But now it shone bright silver, as if new, and the pattern was clear; it contained the image of a dragon, curled around and eating its own tail. Séamus also noticed that he had a small, sturdy-looking dagger in a belt around his waist. There were no pockets in his trews and no sign of his penknife.

He looked in bewilderment at his companion and tried to form a question, but he did not know where to begin. So much was obvious and he could work out easily enough what must have taken place. And yet, could he believe what his senses and his logic were telling him? It is one thing to say, "Ah yes. I see the sky is green and the plants are blue," but it is another to believe it when you have always known the opposite to be true. Fortunately, Séamus did not have such drastic colour changes to contend with, but there were some difficult and personal anomalies to explain nonetheless.

Johnny recognized the predicament that Séamus was in of course. So he did his best to state the obvious and reassure Séamus that his senses were not deceiving him, also filling in the gaps where the explanations were less readily apparent.

"Séamus. Yes, it is I, as you are no doubt already aware. I am more or less as I was when I first crossed into your world following Nuada in his bold expedition."

"And we are both... um?"

"We are both back in my world, yes. The Otherworld to you, perhaps even a land of youth for you, if you were to stay. You opened a path; that was the mist that came so suddenly upon us. I merely guided us along and when I felt I was back where I belonged, I stepped away and the path closed."

Séamus nodded, but said nothing.

"The change was a little painful, and personal," added Johnny after a moment, "I'm sorry if you were a little confused as a result. But don't worry. It's usual to be a bit disorientated making such a journey as this, especially after all that power you conjured up! I knew you had it in you Séamus!"

Séamus kept nodding and looked again over his new apparel, feeling it and examining it. His silent puzzlement demanded further explanation from his companion.

"You have only crossed the boundaries between worlds for the first time, Séamus," continued Johnny. "Naturally, your physical appearance will not have changed at all, why should it? But your clothing and other belongings will be altered to suit your new surroundings, so to speak. This is part of the magic, if it can be called that, over which there is no control. Unless you truly are a powerful sorcerer! Anything you have that would be alien to this world, your watch for example, this will be changed also."

It was at these words that Séamus snapped out of his befuddled state. His watch reminded him of the time, and the time reminded him that he had to get back to his grandfather at The Tavern. Séamus pulled back his cloak to take a look at his left wrist where his watch should have been. The place was now taken up with a tan leather band, decorative and protective, tight but comfortable so that he had hardly noticed it was on. The pattern on the top when he looked at it resembled a sundial, but it certainly could no longer tell him the time.

"It's early afternoon in Spring, judging by the position of the Sun," said Johnny with amusement, "I was away so long that I doubt I've come back at exactly the time I would have wanted. I do feel a bit older, but it's close enough I think. They seem like the same villages down below." He nodded his head at the little hamlet of buildings dotted below the mountain, nestling amongst the valleys of the new hills that had appeared in the Otherworld.

"Fine," said Séamus, finding his voice again. "That's wonderful. Can I go home now?"

Johnny became serious again, not wanting to upset Séamus. He was obviously suffering from feelings of displacement that were in danger of overwhelming him.

"Of course you can go home," Johnny said. "I know of a path the other way in my own country only a couple of days from here. Now you've travelled once, it will be easy."

Then he added quickly, seeing the look of dismay forming upon Séamus's face, "You will remember the time exactly when you left and get back there as if nothing had happened. After only a day or two have passed here your instinct for your own place in your own world will not be distorted, fear not. I may be a few years out, hopefully not too many, because I was gone for centuries. You will be fine. Relax, Séamus. Enjoy your time here."

Séamus paced around, trying to breathe steadily and relax as he was bidden. Of course everything would be alright. Johnny had promised no harm would come to him, and he felt that he knew Johnny was sincere in his promises and that he could believe what he had been told. Hadn't he wanted this adventure, a chance to see another world? He had not realised he would be here for a couple of days, rather than a few minutes or hours, but wasn't that better? A chance to explore and experience a country where so few, if anybody, would ever get the opportunity again?

With an effort, Séamus managed to suppress the feelings of uneasiness that he had with the arrangements as they stood. Johnny had not said that the path back was in a different location, two days' travel away, when he had persuaded Séamus to help. Would he have still come if he had known? Perhaps not, he had to concede, but he was still angry that Johnny had been so economical with the truth and had kept this information secret. There was no point in recriminations though; he relied on Johnny to get him home and he had to trust him. Johnny may have forgotten this detail or even thought it too unimportant to mention. He was sure to say one or the other if Séamus challenged him on the subject anyway.

No, there was nothing to gain by bringing it up. Events were not going as he had expected, but he felt that if he stayed calm, he could influence them and remain in control. He could see to it himself that he did get home.

"When will we set off then?" asked Séamus.

"Soon," answered Johnny cautiously, as if he had been reading Séamus's thoughts, "After I've seen the Druid, the local magician."

"I just want to make sure of how things are in the area, check exactly where the old path lies, that kind of thing," he continued.

This new, unexpected, information threw Séamus once more into a state of consternation.

"The Druid? Check where the path is? I thought you knew that! And you're magic – what do you need a Druid for?" he blurted out.

I'm afraid he had failed to stay calm and in control as he had intended for very long. He realised it too, and blushed in annoyance.

"Whisht! Whisht! Calmly, Séamus! You must take things in more calmly," rebuked Johnny, holding his hands up to appeal for peace, much as he had done before in the Round Field.

"I have no strong powers, magic as you call it, here. You are more likely to have them than me, as I told you before. There are those we call Druids though, and they have powers and knowledge here that surpasses all others. They are independent, but tend to live within the demesne of a chieftain or rulers who they support, in return for mutual protection. As a consequence, they know much of the land of that demesne and of the neighbouring countries."

Whilst he had Séamus attentive and interested, Johnny did not pause. The more Séamus knew and understood, the more he found his balance, his sense of reason in this new world. And Johnny saw that Séamus was already adapting to his surroundings, remarkably quickly.

"A few hundred yards behind you, down the hill a little, you see the high hedge?"

"Yes," said Séamus turning. He had glimpsed it earlier, in the opposite direction to where the bay used to be, but it was only one small detail in the multitude of differences to the landscape that had first assailed him. It had hardly registered at the time as a result, but it had his full attention now.

"It is the boundary to a Druid's garden. They seldom move, so I'm sure he is still here, and I once met and spoke with him. He is not ill disposed towards guests or me in particular. We'll pay him a visit, and I'm sure after you've talked to him, your mind will be set at rest."

Séamus nodded once more and consented to see the Druid.

Unfortunately, as you will see, Johnny could not have been more wrong.

Chapter 8

The Magician in the Garden

They walked down towards the hedge from the summit. It was farther away than Séamus had thought at first, principally because the hedge was far higher than he thought. It was as high as a house, and now that Séamus was up next to it, he realised that it curved around gradually and that it was a circular boundary.

The ground had flattened out where the hedge stood, but a few metres from it, in every direction bar the one facing the summit from which they had come, the ground dropped steeply again.

They walked around the hedge, Johnny first, going clockwise in search of the way in. Séamus assumed Johnny knew where the entrance was. He patiently accompanied him in silence, although he would have liked to have heard the occasional word of encouragement like "Nearly there now" or "Just around the next bit." None were forthcoming though.

In fact, the hedge circle was so big that nearly a quarter of an hour had elapsed before Séamus guessed that they must be about half way round. The fact that no entrance had appeared still made him question whether his companion did indeed know where he was going. If the entrance was on the other side of the hedge, why hadn't Johnny set off anti-clockwise instead? Did he fancy a walk or something?

Séamus held his tongue though at the sight of his companion. Johnny strode purposefully on, his chin set out proudly, daring a question to be asked or a doubt to be raised. Séamus knew that, when you were supposed to know your way somewhere, but got it wrong, the last thing you needed was somebody letting you know what you were already aware of and embarrassed about. This was Johnny's world, but he'd been away for centuries and may have erred in the timing of his return. It was best to forbear and allow Johnny some leeway.

However, he thought a little differently when they came back again in sight of the summit. They had nearly completed the full circuit of the hedge without so much as a gap between the leaves and branches. He managed to come up with a neutral question, one that did not throw any doubt upon his friend's ability.

"Has he made it a magic entrance now then? Is that why we can't see it?"

Johnny grimaced and chewed on his lip for a second before answering.

"I don't know, Séamus, and that's the truth," he said. "The entrance was never hidden before that I heard of, and it was grand enough. I fancied it faced eastwards, so I walked that way at first, then I thought I must have been mistaken and I kept going. But there is nothing. Perhaps he has gone after all."

Johnny stopped abruptly as a clicking metallic sound caught his ear. It seemed to be coming away around the hedge again, clockwise near where they had begun their walk, but just out of sight around the curve. Séamus had heard it too. Johnny instantly strode off in the direction of the sound, Séamus more cautiously at his heels. The sight that greeted him was one that he certainly would not have expected.

An oldish man, tall and upright, stood on a small ladder with his arms above his head, clipping the hedge. He had a straw hat, a check shirt with a waistcoat over it, brown corduroy trousers and wellington boots. In addition to his modern dress, the hedge trimmers looked like something you would buy in a garden centre.

He turned to face them, lowering the clippers and descending the ladder. He had a kind face, more youthful than the bushy white hair and short grey beard had at first made him appear.

"Well, well," he said, in a resonant, slightly threatening tone that belied his pleasant expression. "Visitors from another land, another world we might almost say eh? That doesn't happen very often these days."

Johnny bowed slightly and addressed the gardener.

"It has taken me a long time to come back – I was too late deciding, and then I was lost to this world. With the aid of this excellent boy though," Johnny indicated Séamus with a glance, "I was able to return at last.

"I am known to you, Hartspell," he continued, "Díarmuid, brother to Eremil, Prince of the realm of the Dragon on your borders. I come to ask for tales of my land since I have departed, and for your assistance in finding the path to send my companion back to his world, for I am deeply in his debt."

Johnny bowed again after his declaration was complete. The gardener eyed him coolly for a moment.

"I see no deception in your words," he said at last. "You may enter."

Séamus could hold his tongue no longer. In a rush, he fired questions at the Druid as if he had suddenly found him clipping the whitethorn hedge in front of his own house.

"Are you the Druid? You look like you belong in my world. And why is it so rare for people to travel here – will I be able to get home at all?" he blurted out all at once.

"And you? Díarmuid? What's going on?" he added facing Johnny once more.

Johnny turned slightly away, embarrassed by the lack of etiquette in addressing the Druid, but Séamus was not to know these things, and there was nothing to be done now. He began to form an answer himself, but the Druid interrupted.

There was a look of amusement in his eyes as he replied evenly and with a friendlier tone.

"I am Hartspell, a Druid indeed. If I am *the* Druid, I know not, though I suspect your friend here was seeking no other. As for my garments, it touches on the answer to your other question. Few have the desire, and fewer still the power or the knowledge to move between worlds. I sometimes do still, mostly because your world has an excellent and fascinating selection of equipment and clothing for gardening. I am a very keen gardener you know."

"As for you going home," he continued, "the sooner the better in my opinion or you'll be besieging me with interrogations. If you got here, you can get back, unless you wait too many centuries, like some I could mention."

Hartspell frowned deeply, first at Séamus and then at Johnny, or Díarmuid, as we should perhaps call him now, as he completed his reply. Both were given the impression as the Druid spoke, like a thought implanting itself in their minds, that they were chided, though not seriously, and that they should keep their counsel and only talk if they had something important to say; that is to say, if they were addressed by the Druid himself.

The Druid caught Díarmuid's eye then and, as if he had been given permission, Díarmuid answered the rest of Séamus's question.

"Yes. My name is Díarmuid here. You didn't think I was really called Johnny the Pookie did you?" he laughed. "That title was fine for what I had become in your world. But here, if you please, Díarmuid would be preferable. My brother is ruler of a neighbouring land to this one, Dragonsrealm we call it, and a prince we call him. Eremil is his name and he will order much feasting on my return, so don't head off too soon!"

He clapped a hand on Séamus's back and they both turned towards the Druid, smiling and somewhat relieved, at ease for the first time in a while. The expression on the Druid's face forestalled them though. He looked at them gravely.

"You had better come in. There is much that must be told," he said.

Waving an arm and muttering under his breath, Hartspell stepped forward towards the hedge.

Instantly, two things happened. The first was that the Druid was now wearing a grey cloak and black boots, much more in keeping with the appearance of his two visitors. In fact, Séamus thought that apart from the hat, which was a disappointing round cap rather than a large pointy affair, he looked every inch a powerful magician that you might read about in a fairy tale.

The second was that two large, intricately carved, iron gates appeared and swung inwards noiselessly to open between two huge trees, as high as the hedge. One was an ash and the other a rowan, making Séamus think of the outcrop in the Round Field, but here their branches wove about each other above the top of the gates so that it became impossible to tell where one ended and the other began.

The patterns on the gates seemed to move when Séamus looked at them and tried to make sense of them. At once, they were people, warriors in combat. Then they blurred and became creatures, animals Séamus recognised, and some he did not. For a moment, Séamus thought he saw a dragon, then a woman playing a harp, but as soon as his eye alighted on a figure that it recognised, that figure would change again and he lost any meaning that they might have.

Inside, the grounds were magnificent. The house that itself sat in the middle of the grounds was modest enough in size, but resembled a small, gothic style, castle. The gardens around were also stunning.

They walked on a central path, which lead to the main entrance of the Druid's abode. They initially had to go over an arched bridge across a stream, more like a little river, that ran before them and disappeared into the ground where it met a group of carved granite boulders, before a section of the hedge to their left. The origin of the river was obscured as it wound away to the right and behind the house towards another section of hedge. The trees that lined the river, willows, hazel, rowans and alders, merged with gorse, fuchsia, hawthorn, bog myrtle and other wild shrubs and bushes in an attractive and engaging manner. Consequently, after a couple of turns the route of the meandering river was no longer visible other than by the vegetation that bordered it.

Each side of the river, and to the left and the right of the path, and onwards beyond the house, there were a multitude of other features to delight the eye. There were huge Scots pine, larch, yew, sycamore, horse chestnut and both evergreen and deciduous varieties of oak, dotted here and there over smooth, luscious lawns, adorned with statues and fountains. Flowerbeds and rockeries adorned other areas on either side, a myriad of colours, textures and patterns to make the visual senses dance. The scents of the plants and the sweet noise of a variety of song-birds assailed them so that they walked along almost as if drunk; uncomprehending of their surroundings, enraptured with its beauty, having to concentrate on putting one foot in front of the other.

An orchard was set not far from the right or west side of the house, all trees seemingly in fruit just as all flowers seemed to be in bloom. It was as if the seasons meant nothing here, all creatures and plants were as their host wished them to be. A massive herb garden stretched out of view on the left of the house, seeming to continue behind it. The aromas coming from either side of them were bewitching and uplifting. Séamus reckoned that there were more varieties of herbs in just the portion of the garden that he could see than he could possibly have named or identified. He was put in mind of another story about the Tuatha de Danaan that his father had read to him, about the famous physician Dian Cecht.

Bres had become king of the Tuatha de Danaan, as Nuada had lost an arm when they had been forced to fight the Fir Bolgs for dominion in Ireland, a race settled there when they had first arrived. Bres was known as Bres the Beautiful as he was so handsome, and Nuada could no longer be accepted as ruler being marred in appearance by losing a limb. But Bres had a Fomorian father, the race of monsters and men that lived on islands to the West of Ireland, ruled by Balor of the Evil Eye. He taxed his people heavily and forced them to pay a huge tribute to the Fomorians. The Tuatha de Danaan wished for Nuada to be king again, and so the physician Dian Cecht fashioned a silver arm for Nuada that worked as good as the real limb had. Nuada of the Silver Arm was whole again and delighted by the use of his new arm, but he was still not deemed perfect and could not be king.

It was then that Dian Cecht's son, Miach, took Nuada's embalmed arm that he had lost and worked for nine days to restore it in place of the silver arm. Nuada was then able to be king, but Dian Cecht was so jealous at being surpassed in skill by his son that he killed Miach in a rage and buried him near Tara.

The next day, herbs sprung up around the mound where Miach lay, outlining his body, including every organ, bone and sinew, each herb with special powers connected to the part of the body that it revealed. There were three hundred and sixty-five herbs in all and Airmed, who came to grieve for her brother Miach, attempted to gather and collect them, recording their healing properties. Her jealous father, Dian Cecht, grabbed her cloak and scattered the herbs however, so they could not be sorted out again. To this day as a result, nobody properly understands all the healing powers of the herbs.

Séamus thought at the sight of this garden that somebody must have got very close to gathering all the herbs together again. Did this Druid know as much as Miach and Airmed he wondered?

Then, at last, they approached the Druid's home at the end of the path, lined for the final hundred yards with majestic, leafy elm trees. Two large oak-panelled arched doors opened before them unbidden, and they stepped into the Druid's house.

Chapter 9

The Lost Prince

Inside the light was gloomy; torches suspended on the walls were the only illumination, the interior decoration in keeping with the exterior. It was like the inside of a small stone castle, alcoves situated here and there, a large stone staircase heading up to a landing with a balcony stretching all around the upper floor. The Druid lead them to the right and into a spacious chamber with a low ceiling that was designed to accept guests. A square wooden table was in front of them, laden with fruits, breads, cold meat and bottles of wine and ale. These were accompanied with three plates and drinking vessels as if the Druid had prepared for their arrival.

At the far end of the room, a fire burned brightly giving extra light. Otherwise, the room was illuminated only by two small, narrow windows above them on their right and a flaming torch, set into the wall on their left. Tapestries of woodland scenes and a couple of suits of armour arrayed the walls at the edges of the near rectangular chamber, slightly shorter in width at the far end where the large stone fireplace and surrounding flagstones dominated. The floor, apart from the area before the fire, was almost all covered by a thick, patterned burgundy-coloured rug, the patterns as elusive as those in the gates to the garden, though thankfully stationary.

The Druid motioned his guests to sit around the table. The three large, leather-covered chairs around it were the only furniture save for bookcases either side of the fireplace, full of big, old, dusty looking tomes. As he sat, Séamus looked up at some of the shields and weapons that also decorated the walls in the gaps between the tapestries and the two armour sentinels.

"It is nearly a hundred years since you departed. The paths between worlds are well-nigh no more," began the Druid, addressing Díarmuid without preamble.

Díarmuid looked stunned, he had thought it would be a couple of decades at the most. How could he have got it so wrong? He had no time to think however, before the Druid continued in ominous tones.

"Your brother is no longer alive, although sadly it was not age that defeated him."

Díarmuid now sat rigid in his chair, staring at the Druid. He was partly afraid of the story he was to hear, yet desperate to know the events that had befallen in the long period of his absence. The Druid sensed his apprehension, but did not shirk from continuing with the rest of his tale.

"No heir of Eremil rules on Dragonshill now. These are darker times and alas, the ruler of this land and others neighbouring your own do not act but for their own defence. It is indeed fortunate, and no coincidence I think, that you have come when you have, and not earlier. Those that rule in your family's stead no longer look to your return; they sit in comfort and complacency as they abuse your land. Your people still hope for the return of The Lost Prince, for now, Díarmuid, it is you that bears that title. And it is you who must rid Dragonsrealm of the tyranny that corrupts and engulfs it."

Saying this, the Druid rose, and lifted from behind Díarmuid a weapon that had lain in shadow on the wall behind him, beneath one of the windows. It was a greatsword, a huge two-handed blade as long as Séamus himself. At the hilt, the large leather-wrapped handle bore a bright silver emblem in the centre. It was the emblem of a dragon, circled around, eating its own tail. The same as the pattern on Séamus's brooch.

"How came you by this?" demanded Díarmuid, standing and grabbing the proffered sword.

Hartspell sighed. "I was there, I was there," he said softly and sadly.

His tone made Díarmuid sit again, clasping the sword to his chest. "Go on," he said, shaking.

"It was not many years after your sister was lost and you departed with Nuada when Stormspell, the Druid that resided in your land, older than you or I could reckon, decided his time had come and he must return to the Earth. He said farewell to your brother and set off Northwards to where he alone knew, and to his final rest. Many lands exist comfortably and peacefully without the assistance of a Druid, and Eremil did not look for a replacement to the aged sage who had been like a father to him. Aye, and to you Díarmuid," added Hartspell, taking a sip of wine before continuing.

"But a replacement did present himself, a stranger travelling down from the North whence Stormspell had flown but six years before. He was young, keen and powerful, charismatic and well liked by all at court on Dragonshill. Some said that Eremil had his brother back again in this boon companion and Wolfspell, for so he was called, became the Druid in your land. It was two years after that when Lokil came."

The Druid had paused as if building up courage for the rest of the tale. Séamus and Díarmuid both sat still, tense in anticipation of what was to come. The unspoken question of "Who is Lokil?" filled the air, as the Druid resumed.

"Lokil was, is, an ice giant. He stands nearly as high as the hedge that surrounds my gardens, the height of three full-grown men. Why he has come out of his home in the Ice Mountains beyond the North no one can tell. But he came, and he came with followers. He has some magic and a desire for power, and he installed the desire for a kingdom into those who flocked to his cause. Men, beasts of the forests, some whom we would term monsters, formed an army that encamped beneath the centre of your brother's land, at the base of Dragonshill itself. Lokil declared that Dragonsrealm was now his and bade Eremil to become his vassal. Eremil answered him as was fitting. The unknown approach of the giant's army had cut him off from many who would have joined him. But with the retinue of his castle and the creatures of the mountain of Dragonshill itself, he set forth to confront and defeat Lokil, Wolfspell at his side."

The Druid had paused again. His expression was as one looking back through time, recalling traumatic events and recoiling from the horror.

Díarmuid could not contain himself anymore. "How do you know all this? How was the day lost? Eremil had the higher ground and the Druid!"

"Ah," sighed Hartspell, "Much have I learned since that day from those who witnessed what occurred. And much I saw for myself. A great feeling of foreboding, of the imminent doom of a friend, had overcome me, and I reached out with my feelings, and the centre of this doom lay over the rath of Eremil, the fort on Dragonshill. I watched from here, with a vision spell, what happened from that point onwards. I saw the forces arrayed, Eremil above and Lokil below.

"The giant's forces were greater, but the position favoured your brother. It was then that my forebodings were explained. Lokil raised his club to begin the assault, and Wolfspell struck. Not at the giant, but at your brother's army."

Díarmuid was on his feet again in fury, but he did not interrupt.

"The shock and the consternation as fire and wind assailed them from within put Eremil's forces into disarray long enough for Lokil's army to close the gap between the forces. All advantages that Eremil had were now gone. The giant, with the Druid and the greater numbers in his host, not to mention his own power, were routing your brother's forces. He shouted for them to save themselves and retreat, whilst he fought valiantly with a circle of knights to attract the main force of his enemy.

"I left then, as swiftly as I could on a cloud, and I arrived minutes later at the battlefield. Eremil's knights were splintered and he was overrun with foes as I landed and scattered those about him. He bade me take his sword, saying his life was lost, and asked me to help redeem his land. The giant and Wolfspell were not long in turning their attentions to me and I felt their power, both trying to hold me in a binding spell. The giant's magic was negligible next to mine, like a grain of sand on a beach, but added to that of Wolfspell, it nearly made all the difference. I was able to depart again as I had come, bearing your brother's sword, but I could not bring his body. Since then, I have done what I can to strengthen the borders of my sovereign's land, though there is no sign of ambition for further territory yet in the giant. And I have awaited your return, for no one else will come forward to deliver Dragonsrealm and avenge your brother."

Heavily, the Druid returned to his seat. Séamus sat quietly and respectfully, trying to take in the implications for Díarmuid, having for the moment forgotten his own predicament. Díarmuid sat with a tear in his eye, gripping the sword tightly with a burning anger in his face. It was an altered, murderous look that made him appear more fearful to Séamus then than Johnny the Pookie had ever been.

Throughout the rest of the day, Díarmuid gleaned as much information as he could from Hartspell. Séamus tagged along, trying to offer helpful suggestions every now and again, not wanting to be forgotten.

To his relief, and a little to his surprise, both Díarmuid and the Druid not only tolerated his interruptions, they gave his thoughts serious consideration and respected his opinion. Séamus added weight to the Druid's own conviction that for Díarmuid to go in and challenge the giant to single combat or to attempt to raise an army to defeat the usurpers was unrealistic. The former relied on the chivalrous acceptance of the giant, which was very unlikely, not to mention the fact that beating him in single combat would be, "forgive the pun", Séamus said, "a very tall order".

The latter could not be done quickly or secretly and would give time for the enemy to prepare and, most likely, put more of them into the field in better, defensive positions. The only option that seemed to remain, Séamus stated thinking aloud, was to gather a small party quickly to seize Eremil's rath, on Dragonshill, whilst the occupiers were ignorant of their approach. In the meantime they would send word to would-be supporters that the Lost Prince had returned. An army could be made ready to defend the stronghold once retaken, hopefully before Lokil or Wolfspell could muster their forces to make an attempt upon it.

As Séamus stopped his musing and looked up to hear the response of his two elders, picking out the flaws and weaknesses of his strategy, he saw them both looking at him in admiration. There was a small grin on the Druid's face, a look of determination and pride on Díarmuid's.

"That's settled then," Díarmuid said.

"Well done, Séamus," added Hartspell. "No doubt we would have got to the same conclusion eventually. But you do seem to have a talent for clear military thinking. Perhaps that is your gift in this world, hmm?"

He then turned to Díarmuid.

"We can prepare provisions this evening, and we will leave early on the morrow."

Díarmuid bowed, and signalled for Séamus to follow him to a room that the Druid had prepared for them. Séamus did not know what to think. This was turning into more of an adventure than he had bargained for.

*

In the morning, backpacks ready, they set off down the mountain towards the first of the little villages in the valleys.

Hartspell had recalled that, after the battle, many of Eremil's followers had fled the borders of his realm, the remainder left in hiding or in serfdom still within it. He thus hoped that within the edges of his own land of Cruachan Aille they would thus find those who would aid their cause. Both Díarmuid and Séamus were very glad indeed that the Druid also considered it his cause and was coming with them, for now that they had started on their road, doubts inevitably began to crowd their thoughts.

Based on the Druid's reasoning, they had not departed from the mountain top too early, but mid-morning so as to arrive in the village in the early afternoon. This way, they hoped to find as many people out and about in the village as possible. After less than two hours, they rounded a bend in the path that led eastwards down from the summit, the ground already becoming more even and easier to travel.

In the valley now, the first of the houses of the little hamlet was before them, the rest not too far beyond. People were indeed abroad in numbers. Séamus felt a nervous sensation in the pit of his stomach as he trailed after the Druid and Díarmuid, who both walked confidently into the heart of the village.

Chapter 10

Díarmuid gets a Raiding Party

The village was made up of small stone houses; some with turf roofs, some with thatched roofs, some square, some round. Small windows and open doorways were the norm, with smoke rising from a single central chimney in the majority. They were not positioned in any particular pattern, but seemed to focus on a large, central open square. This was evidently a market square where many people could be seen now buying or selling assorted produce; animals, fodder, clothes, food, tools and even some weapons.

Other people were at work maintaining some of the houses, or in the adjacent fields. Children ran about outside a rather large oblong, well-thatched, building that Séamus took to be a school. There must have been a break in the lessons, or else they finished earlier here.

Some people were dressed in a manner similar to themselves, but most wore plainer garments, rustic brown or greys, tough clothes to be comfortable in whilst working and resting. Some of the children were bare-foot, but it seemed to be by choice. There was neither obvious opulence nor poverty. It seemed a well-organised, contented village.

Many now stopped what they were doing as they watched Hartspell and his two companions enter the market square. Some nodded or hailed the Druid with words of greetings. But everyone waited for him to speak. It was obvious that the Druid had come down among them for a reason, and they wanted to know what it was.

What followed can be easily summarised. The Druid presented the Lost Prince and his servant, returned to reclaim the kingdom of Dragonsrealm. All wished them well, but only a dozen men and women who had come out of that land, or were the sons and daughters of those who had been forced to flee from the original battle, pledged themselves to follow Díarmuid and to defeat Lokil the giant. Séamus thought this very few, but hid his disappointment, as both Díarmuid and the Druid seemed well pleased. They had clearly expected no better, perhaps worse.

"This is a good beginning," declared Hartspell as they ate before continuing their journey. Horses had been found for all, some belonged to the followers, and the Druid purchased others. Séamus sat atop a fine horse that was just his size, reminding him of a Connemara pony that he had seen in a fair at Clifden, a mare called Misty.

"I think I shall call you Misty," he whispered in the horse's ear as he mounted her, ready to continue the journey. The horse nodded enthusiastically as if well pleased with her name and Séamus wondered if she could actually understand him.

He did not have much time to consider this or put it to the test once mounted though. Introductions were made and then Díarmuid wanted to commence the journey forthwith.

Of the twelve new companions, three were female – Cliona, Fionnuala and Emer. Séamus thought that Emer looked little older than he was himself, though she was far more confident on a horse than he, and she faced no opposition when she volunteered to join the company. The nine men were called Cian, Cormac, Donall, Dafydd, Jarlath, Niall, Corey, Brannan and Cet. Brannan looked to be late middle-aged, but had said that he was a boy when his father fought against Lokil, so that Séamus could only assume that the inhabitants of the Otherworld did themselves enjoy some of the benefits attributed to the Land of Youth.

The party now headed straight for the low hills that marked the beginning of Dragonsrealm. A couple of the men that had joined them detoured to take in a few of the other nearby villages so see if any more would accompany them. They would have to catch the others up. It was important for the main party to head straight for their destination now that the tidings of Díarmuid's return were abroad, lest by some mishap that the news would be spread too rapidly and would reach the rath on Dragonshill before them.

At nightfall, they set up camp; horses and provisions in the centre with people sleeping placed several feet distant around them at regular intervals. Each of the ten remaining recruits who had followed Díarmuid from the village took turns at keeping a watch in pairs. This worked out at only just over an hour each, as they intended to set off again not long after dawn. Consequently, most of them got a good night's sleep in an uneventful night.

Díarmuid himself slept the whole time, the first proper rest he had had since returning to his world. He had barely managed a sleep at all the previous night at the Druid's home. Séamus had also been told to try to sleep the whole night through; both Díarmuid and Hartspell expressing the view that he had been through what must be a multitude of new and strange experiences in the last twenty-four hours already. There was no need for him to concern himself with a watch while they were still outside the borders of Dragonsrealm; they expected all watches that night to remain undisturbed.

The Druid himself appeared to be awake all the time though, Séamus noticed, and Séamus himself slept in fits and starts, despite his best efforts. He was unused to sleeping in the open, even though the blanket from the backpack provided by the Druid was amazingly comfortable. Combined with the springy heather, this took most of the stiffness out of sleeping on hard ground. However, it could not silence the multitude of noises that you hear when outside in the countryside at night, nor could it prevent the many new experiences and concerns competing for notice in Séamus's mind.

When they began their journey again in the morning, Séamus was thus still quite tired, and he half dozed on Misty's back as they travelled over the easy terrain. As noon approached however, he was well rested and fully awake, when the first of the two riders, Brannan, came back into view and approached them cutting along tracks through the surrounding cultivated fields.

He was not alone. With him was a woman, about Díarmuid's height, which was nearly six feet tall, dark skinned, beautiful, Séamus thought, and on perhaps the biggest steed he had ever seen. This must be what they call a war-horse, he thought, and indeed, parts of the horse were protected by metal plate armour, decorative like that of its rider. Both she and Brannan dismounted as they reached the leading horses of Díarmuid and Hartspell.

"Plenty of good wishes, but no more followers from yonder village," said Brannan to Díarmuid. "Apart from this Free Knight, from overseas," he added, "who offers her services."

"For a commensurate reward of course. I am Meeshan," said the woman, smiling, her head held proudly as she met Díarmuid's eye. Her accent was broad, and Séamus wondered if she had called herself 'Mission', and he pondered what her mission might be. Something about her bearing told him it was a question he should keep to himself though.

Apart from the armour, a large breastplate with intricate spiral designs, a segmented metal skirt around her abdomen, and leather and metal vambraces, greaves and cuisses covering her lower and upper arms and legs, she seemed to carry an arsenal of weapons. In a belt around her waist hung a broadsword in a scabbard and two daggers, one curved and one straight. A quiver of arrows was strapped around her back; the bow hung from one of the horse's saddlebags accompanied by a lance, a mace and a shield. There was also a helmet hung on the horse's side, plain enough with a nasal and cheek guards for frontal protection, apart from a wicked looking pointed boss positioned on the forehead that Séamus imagined could only be for giving somebody the mother of all head-butts.

She carried in her hands at the moment a long wooden staff, which she rested on the ground as if it were a walking stick. But the metal, studded ends belied this. Séamus did not doubt that if Díarmuid or the Druid said the wrong thing to her, she would reach them easily up on their horses with her quarterstaff, for it was clearly a weapon, if she had a mind to wield it.

"We are glad to have you with us," said Díarmuid shortly, with a small bow in his saddle, no doubt himself having taken in all that Séamus had noted and more besides.

As they rode on, Séamus moved up besides Díarmuid to raise a couple of points that had been bothering him since Meeshan had joined them. She had chosen for herself a position guarding the rear of the party, which rode more or less in file, two at a time where their route allowed, so there was no danger of her overhearing.

"Díarmuid, what is a Free Knight? She mentioned reward. Isn't she just a mercenary?" he asked. The Druid raised his eyebrows at this, but said nothing as Díarmuid responded.

"It is different here, Séamus. Much is thought of feats in arms, though wanton slaughter is of course condemned. Where some may not be content with the military opportunities afforded to them in their own land, or simply have no opportunity for plying their trade where their realm is long at peace, they may decide to offer their services to other kingdoms. Or they may have to leave for other reasons. Who can say what Meeshan's reasons were, it has no bearing on us. She has given her service to no ruler in particular, but has chosen to be a Free Knight, to follow others into adventure and live off the rewards and obtain the glory she craves from such encounters. From her bearing, appearance, and the quality of her arms, she is successful in her career. Free Knights such as her are much admired, and rightly so."

Séamus thought on this for a moment, but was still troubled. "But she could offer her services to anyone. Had she been across the border of your land, she may have offered it to our enemy. How can that be good?"

Díarmuid flashed an angry glance at Séamus. "Free Knights are not without principle. It would be a poor bearer of the title that gave service to a usurper and a tyrant. They live by reputation and would get little business elsewhere if that were the case. One or two here have heard of Meeshan. They alerted me to her reputation as she approached. Do not let her know of your doubts in her character, Séamus, she would take it ill."

Séamus nodded. "I'm sorry. I just don't understand how everything works here yet," he said. His tone was not too apologetic though, as he had felt it was a fair question and something that he had needed to understand.

It was enough to placate Díarmuid however, who had relaxed again.

"There is more, I judge by your look, that you would ask?" he said to Séamus in a more humorous tone.

"Yes. I noticed it with the Druid," he nodded at Hartspell who had now dropped back in the line as their track had narrowed, "but I assumed it was some magic of his. But it is the same with Meeshan as well. She speaks and I understand her, but when I see her lips move, I think she is talking another language. How do I hear it in my own tongue, or is it all the Druid's doing?"

Díarmuid smiled a broad grin at this and looked Séamus in the eye.

"Magic? No, it is no trick, that is simply how it is here. Your ears interpret sounds, so you know if you hear glass breaking, or a cat mewing. And with language this means you understand what is said to you. What is strange is that this does not happen in your own world. It is as if the part of your brain that translates to understanding the sound of speech has been locked away. What is the point of hearing someone speak and not knowing what it is they are saying?" he looked askance at Séamus. "It makes it very difficult for us when we go to your world you know. I can understand them, but I have to learn to speak in their tongue for them to understand me! That's why I didn't travel much, just communicating could give me a headache."

"But how come I can understand now when I couldn't before? Will I be able to understand every language when I go back?" Séamus continued.

"That I can't answer because I don't know. Your garments have changed to fit in with this world when you crossed over. There may have been an adjustment in your mind also. Who can say? And what you will retain when you return – I can't answer that either. I should imagine you would return as you have left, as I have here, but only time will tell, my friend."

Séamus, for the first time since Díarmuid had heard of Eremil's death, felt able now to raise the subject to his friend of his return home again. Díarmuid seemed more at ease and approachable once more, and the conversation had turned to give Séamus the opening he needed to voice his concern.

"You do still plan to find me the path back then? When you've sorted this business out of course. It's just, well, if things don't go according to plan. I'm worried that's all, worried that I'll be trapped here forever."

Díarmuid was quiet for a moment and he looked ahead steadily, weighing his answer. At last, he sighed and said gently to Séamus. "This task I must do. But if it goes well or ill, I will do all I can to make sure that you go home. If I do not survive this, the Druid likely will, he knows my debt to you and will see it paid." He turned to face Séamus again.

"You are a brave lad, and you have shown much forbearance in accepting what has befallen. You could not have been blamed for screaming and protesting like a bairn.

But you speak only of a fear of being trapped, not a fear of being killed or of taking your part in this adventure, for it did not cross your mind. I take heart at that, Séamus, for I feel that the strength is in you to see this through. You will get... hello?"

Díarmuid stopped for, on their left, five figures could be seen approaching a couple of hundred yards away. They came from over the brow of a small hill, in a wide glade between two small copses of mixed birch and pine trees. He leaned forward to take in the approaching figures.

"Very good," he said sounding deeply satisfied. "Four more for our raiding party, and of fine calibre too, or I'm a leprechaun's supper."

Séamus tried to take the figures in. Leading was Jarlath, the other rider who had gone to sound out more villages. Behind him on his right were two shapes that Séamus recognised, but he had to blink twice at them to believe what he was seeing. They had the heads and upper bodies of men, but the lower bodies of a large horse. In other words, they were centaurs.

However, the sight of the two others behind Jarlath on the left was stranger yet. Jogging along in small leather moccasins, with a one-piece brownish plaid wrapped around his body, was a tall man, well over six foot, easily keeping pace with the trotting horse and centaurs with seemingly very little effort. Adjacent to him was a huge long dark creature, scurrying rather than running on all fours, criss-crossed with two thick belts, intersecting diagonally over its rounded body that was full of long sharp quills. Séamus realised, his jaw open in astonishment, that it was a giant-sized hedgehog.

Chapter 11

Two Centaurs, Spiny and Angus Óg the Foot

Meeshan and Hartspell rode to the front of the ranks to join Díarmuid and Séamus as they greeted the new arrivals. The two centaurs were called Crannock and Crellock and they were originally from the forest of Dragonsrealm, beyond the fort and the plain below it. Many centaurs and creatures of the forest had joined Lokil's army, swayed by the giant's promises and by his apparent magical charisma. There were numerous creatures who stayed loyal to Eremil though, most now living beyond the borders of Dragonsrealm, whilst others eked out an existence in hiding deep within the forest still. Crannock and Crellock were brothers, it was difficult to tell them apart, and they seemed to speak as one, completing each other's sentences as they proclaimed their loyalty to Díarmuid's cause.

"We want to atone," said Crannock.

"For the betrayal by our people," said Crellock.

"We wish to join your force and fight," added Crannock again.

"To see a lawful ruler in Dragonshill once more," completed Crellock finally. They both bowed to Díarmuid at this, nervous perhaps of the reception they may get when so many of their kind had deserted and fought for the enemy.

"I am honoured," said Díarmuid readily. "The errors of your people are not yours, and they perhaps rue that decision already. You set the example that will begin the turning of the tide." And he bowed in return.

The centaurs practically whinnied with delight at these fine words. Sharing a glance, but unable to speak for joy, they cantered to the back of the small troop accompanied by Jarlath where they were given some of the spare swords and shields carried by the horses.

Díarmuid now turned to face the other two arrivals. The hedgehog had now stood on its hind legs to reveal not only that it was seven feet high and immensely broad, but also that the insides of the two leather belts that could be seen strapped along the back were laden with swords, axes and daggers. It was clear that this creature was going to speak first, and nobody complained.

"I'm called Spiny, in this form anyway. I'm a shape-shifter, though I haven't shifted shape in quite a while," he said gruffly. "That's because I like it this way, not because I've forgotten how to change back, see. Don't you let anyone tell you different!" he added, raising his voice as he completed his introduction.

"Well, er, Spiny, you are very welcome," said Díarmuid, to break the awkward silence that followed. "And do you wish to join us in our sortie?"

"I wouldn't be here otherwise would I!" responded Spiny, equally as gruffly as before. "I used to live in the big wood same as them horsemen – though they won't know me – but chased out I was. By an army mind! Nothing less would have moved me, and they paid for it hear – there's two score men of that giant who won't be dancing the next time Alara has her skirts full out!"

Séamus looked confused at the end of Spiny's latest expostulation, but Díarmuid and everybody else knew that the hedgehog was referring to the next full moon. Díarmuid remained calm, for the moment unconcerned by the aggressive tones that Spiny adopted when speaking. He recognised it as a trait of the creature rather than any obvious challenge to himself or to his authority.

"Well we are glad to have you with us," he replied. "And your fleet-footed companion is?"

"Scotty, I'll vouch for him. Plays great pipe music and 'e's good in a fight!" blustered Spiny again. The man stood forward.

"Angus Óg at your service. Free Knight and adventurer," he announced, with a cheeky grin and a wink at Meeshan.

It was she who replied before Díarmuid could speak.

"Angus Óg the Foot," she said levelly. "Bounty hunter. Assassin."

Séamus looked over at the new Free Knight in more detail. He still grinned at Meeshan, but there was a menace in his eyes that boded ill.

His garment was indeed a brown plaid, but it was patterned subtly with other colours, purples, reds and greens, in what Séamus could only call a tartan style. It was all the one piece, wrapped over the shoulder and pleated below the waist. Here a thick black studded belt housed a huge one-handed sword, bigger than the broadswords most of them carried, but not so large as the greatsword that Díarmuid had strapped across his back.

"You want to be careful about believing everything ye hear lassie," said Angus at last, easing the tension slightly, but not much.

Díarmuid interrupted and tried to regain control of the situation.

"Angus Óg the Foot? A curious title?" he asked.

Again, Meeshan answered.

"Because he will ride no beast, but can run with them. I've also heard he can resist the magic of Druids and walk unseen. Very useful talents if true, though I've also heard he worked for a vampire in Fomor, the kingdom of shadows."

Angus's eyes fixed on Meeshan once more. This time the smile was gone.

"I'm glad my fame and news of my talents have reached so far," he said with a sarcastic sneer. "I ken not how you come by such knowledge, but I warn ye again. Be careful."

Angus's arms had not moved from his side, but Meeshan's right hand now hovered above her sword, loose in its scabbard on her left side, ready to be drawn quickly across her body. It was now Hartspell who interrupted before Díarmuid could be heard.

"I heard of a tale that a prince of the shadow's realm, a tyrant of great cruelty, was killed on the wishes of a vampire whose territory was threatened by the prince," the Druid said, in a measured tone that demanded attention.

"I also heard," he added, looking now at Angus, "that the vampire himself was killed not long after that."

Angus now grinned again. "I heard something of the kind myself," he laughed. "Lost his head in an argument with a claymore. Apparently yon tyrant and yon bloodsucker both paid very well to have each other removed. So I heard," he finished.

"I'll vouch for him!" barked the hedgehog again.

"Alright," said Díarmuid now, grateful for the Druid's intervention and the easing of tempers. "You wish to join us – I can't promise huge rewards?"

"My needs are quite modest, sometimes," said Angus now, cheerful again.

"My big friend here has been put out of his home. And I don't like ice giants, not down here away from where they should be, neither. No more than I like vampires," Angus concluded with a pointed look at Meeshan who had relaxed her posture but not her look of disdain.

"Very well. We are getting closer to my kingdom, we could do with someone ahead scouting. You won't be easy to see in that outfit, especially without the burden of a mount," said Díarmuid decisively.

Meeshan turned away at this, and headed back towards the end of the troop once more without further comment.

"That's the very idea!" said Angus with another big grin, bowing slightly and, with a careful pat on Spiny's back, disappearing ahead to the right side of the path and into the heather.

Angus kept at about three or four hundred yards ahead of the party in that manner, crossing from left to right, for the rest of the afternoon. He did not tire, despite being on rougher terrain and on foot. Séamus thought that even when the scout was straight ahead of them, with no bends or rises in the ground to obscure his position, he would have been nearly impossible to see had they not known he was there.

Séamus was uneasy about Angus because of Meeshan's reaction; he certainly sounded more like a mercenary than Díarmuid's description of a Free Knight. But Hartspell had turned the confrontation in a way that obtained acceptance for Angus, and Meeshan had not protested once Díarmuid made his decision to include Angus as his scout.

Was her outburst just professional jealousy? Somehow Séamus doubted it, and he feared the Druid and Díarmuid had taken Angus on board so as not to make an enemy out of him, and possibly Spiny too as a consequence. The raiment of the scout had also confused Séamus, the material was somewhat in keeping with the garments of the others, but the style was very different.

The accent was clearly Scottish, Spiny had referred to him as Scotty, and the whole demeanour of the man reminded Séamus of a highland warrior from out of the history books of his own world. A clansman and a raider, dressed in a one-piece simply decorated plaid, multi-coloured depending on what material and dyes were available. This was before modern fashion reduced the highland dress to just a kilt below the waist only, in different regimented colours and patterns that were supposedly clan tartans.

Séamus got closer to Hartspell and Díarmuid who rode together at the head of the line once more. The track they were following had narrowed again, the land now rising more steeply as they began to enter the hills that had seemed so distant at the start of the morning.

"The scout, Angus. Is he from another country?" he asked.

Both turned their heads slightly to look at Séamus.

"He is from your world," answered the Druid. "I thought you would know."

"There is something about him and his clothes. But mine all changed," Séamus replied looking down at what he was wearing. "I don't understand."

"Hmm, I see," said Hartspell. "Well I suppose when he crossed to this world, there wasn't that much difference in how he appeared and how the people of the land he arrived in were dressed. So he stayed as he is. Mostly - it sounds like he has certain talents in this world that are beyond most of us here."

"I told you that you are more likely than I to be magic in this land, Séamus," added Díarmuid.

"Well I don't seem to have any abilities at all," replied Séamus gloomily.

"We shall see, we shall see," said the Druid once more, smiling at Séamus.

"I'm sure that Angus fellow took a long time to adjust and discover what he could do. He has been here a while now judging by his reputation. Do not have a fear of him, Séamus. He has chosen to be a Free Knight and follows the code as well as he can, based on what he was used to in his world. I sense no treachery in him, not for us anyhow."

At that, there was a sudden shout of "Hold!" from the scout, who leapt up close ahead of them, barely two hundred yards away, as if appearing out of the earth. He gestured with a hand signal for the group to ride towards him, and the riders spurred their horses on.

"What have you found?" asked Díarmuid when he reached Angus.

"Just over the brow of that hill," indicated the scout. "There are posts now to mark the boundary into Dragonsrealm. They are topped with skulls, a nice little warning, but it may dishearten some of yon men if you dinnae warn them first."

Díarmuid nodded grimly and gathered the group together where he spoke to them in a low voice, urging them to show their mettle and not be dissuaded by any show of the enemy. All accepted his words, but Spiny, when he heard tell of the skulls, shuffled off at speed over the hill to take a look for himself before the rest of the party moved on again.

A moment later, a roar was heard out of the hedgehog. Díarmuid and his men all rode forward fearing an attack. As they came into view of the great creature though, they saw him tearing down all the posts in a rage, moving along the line of the border with Angus trailing after him and trying to calm him down. Finally, when Díarmuid feared that the hedgehog would carry on out of sight, not stopping until he had demolished the posts along the entire length of the borders of Dragonsrealm, Spiny ceased. He collapsed onto all fours on the ground, breathing heavily.

None moved to bring him back to the group, but allowed him to take his own time accompanied by his confederate the scout. He shuffled towards Meeshan at the rear of the line once more, not saying a word as he returned.

Angus stayed at the front and addressed Díarmuid.

"One skull over the track was that of a very large badger. He kens it must be Brock, another shape-changer he was familiar with." It was the first time that Angus had said anything in a sombre tone without any humour or sarcasm in his voice.

"I'll go back up front now, give me a minute to get in position then follow."

Díarmuid nodded in return. "We'll be stopping in another hour for camp," he said to all. "Let's try and make good time."

They continued along the rough track, between two large standing stones marked with black intersecting lines going from top to bottom. Séamus recognised the markings as

Ogham script, the combinations of horizontal lines crossing a vertical bar at a particular angle representing a letter. It had been used in early history in Ireland and could also be found in some places in neighbouring countries across the sea. He had no idea how to read this script though, but Díarmuid was able to solve that problem for him, reading aloud in an angry tone like a tense whisper as he passed the stones.

"Dragonsrealm. Those that enter my demesne, pay tribute to Lokil," he read.

"We'll see about that."

Chapter 12

Séamus Wins His Spurs

Séamus thought about the skulls he had seen. Some had been of people, some of animals and some of creatures that Séamus did not know. It brought it home to him that here was an adventure where they were gambling their fortune and the stakes were lives. He tried to steel himself and prepare for whatever was to come so that he did not let Díarmuid down.

They moved on cautiously but speedily as the light faded. It would soon be time to make camp and Díarmuid considered calling Angus back, from wherever he was in front of them, when the ambush struck.

Suddenly, from all sides, men with horses rose out of long grass, from behind gorse bushes, from amongst rocks and in other sheltered places where they had been lying in wait. They mounted quickly and before anyone had time to take in what was happening and organise a defence, the riders had opened fire with their bows and unleashed a flurry of arrows.

They were a uniformed cavalry unit, all bearing red cloaks and red helmets over black trews and black boots. Their shields were red and black also, emblazoned with a wolf motif that stared out at their opponents with an open maw. Three men and one of the centaurs, Crellock, went down in the hail of arrows, the others going wide of the mark or bouncing off shield or armour.

If it had not been for this initial blow, the forces would have been more evenly matched, as there were but two dozen in the attacking cavalry. But with four down, the defending band were now only sixteen, fifteen not counting the scout who was nowhere to be seen and must be in hiding. That is, if he had not already been surprised and felled by the force that had been lying in wait.

Díarmuid and his troop were now quick to respond after the opening onslaught. Realising that their position was weak, grouped together by a surrounding foe, but that the enemy were spread thinly around and not huge in numbers, Díarmuid ordered a counter attack. The nine men and women from the village who were still seated and uninjured plus Crannock the Centaur rallied to him and they charged towards the left.

By hitting one half of the circle at first only, they were not at a numerical disadvantage there and it also forced the soldiers attacked on that side to draw swords and abandon their bows. However, the soldiers on the other side of the circle tried to get another barrage of arrows loosened at Díarmuid's offensive group. The Druid had remained where he was though casting spells of protection on the men, so that when the arrows fired at their backs approached them, they seemed to bounce off an invisible armour inches from their target, glowing red as if burnt. This, in addition to the fact that a seven-foot tall armoured hedgehog was now bearing down on them, forced the other dozen soldiers on the right of the track to draw swords also.

Spiny's charge unnerved the horses that he approached. One soldier struggled to regain control of his mount; two others nearby dismounted just in time to meet the hedgehog's attack as he reared onto his hind legs and drew a sword with each forepaw, snarling at his foes beneath him.

The nine others on that side were not incapacitated however, and they had now turned their attention towards the Druid. He was still on the track in the centre of the fight, with Séamus by his side on Misty, wondering what, if anything, he could or should do.

On the left-hand side of the track, fierce close-quarter fighting had now broken out between Díarmuid and his troops and the red soldiers. Séamus thought Díarmuid's group were getting the better of it, but he realised that would soon change if the other soldiers could get past the Druid and assail them from behind. As the nine advanced towards him, and as Séamus wondered what the Druid would do, two things happened simultaneously.

Meeshan, who had quietly and calmly dismounted at the rear of the party when the attack began, walked up the track towards Séamus and Hartspell carrying a crossbow that appeared to have a rotating barrel beneath it. Each section of the barrel housed a bolt and, setting her feet apart steadfast on the ground, she fired at the leading group of cavalry who were riding at the Druid, adjusting her hold deftly as she alternated between targets. Each shot, less than a second apart, cannoned into the riders or their mounts.

Three riders were blown out of their saddles by the impact of the crossbow bolts and two horses were injured so that their riders were forced to dismount else be trapped beneath them as they fell. Without transition, Meeshan then placed the device she had so carefully prepared at her feet and drew her sword, standing a few feet now from Hartspell and ready to intercept foes from his right.

At the same time, from out of nowhere between two of the other riders on that side, further over to the Druid's left, a figure appeared out of the heather and grass, pulling both riders to the ground. There was a flurry of activity and then Angus emerged grinning from the confusion, leaving two motionless bodies behind him.

The two riders who had lost their mounts to Meeshan now ran at her with swords drawn, so that the remaining two who had been furthest away, unscathed by the attacks of Angus or the multi-arrowed crossbow, were now riding straight at Hartspell and Séamus with nobody to intercept them. Séamus did not know if the Druid had any spells that could protect him from the advancing soldiers, but he had a feeling that he must do something to distract at least one of the two approaching assailants, or his friend could be in serious trouble.

Almost without thinking, he heard himself urge Misty on, heading for his opponent with his dagger drawn in his left hand. The rider he approached speeded up his mount also, drawing a broadsword and carrying a shield. His helmet and shield bore an additional black stripe, so Séamus realised he must be going into combat with the leader of the cavalry unit. The visor on his opponent's closed-helmet was lifted, and Séamus saw that he was grinning as he covered the distance towards him, raising his sword ready to strike.

What am I doing, thought Séamus, attacking this soldier with just a dagger on this pony?

He was momentarily even more perplexed when he realised that he had also taken up his weapon in his left hand, when he was right-handed. Yet as his enemy bore down upon him, he suddenly and inexplicably became very clear-headed.

His opponent was too confident; Séamus saw that he would not be able to stay on his horse if hit by a severe jolt when both of his hands were occupied with sword and shield. Misty charged bravely onwards and, in a flash, Séamus pulled back his left arm and flung the dagger with all his might – just before the soldier reached him to deliver his sword-stroke.

The leather sundial design on the strap on his wrist gave a brief golden glow as Séamus released the dagger. He felt as if a warrior instinct had taken possession of him; he remained calm and his aim was true and strong. He felt distant as well; as if he was viewing the scenario from outside, a professional soldier critically weighing-up how one protagonist would outwit the other.

The dagger hit the shield with a force that jolted the rider off his mount, some two yards off the back of his mount to be precise. The dagger had also pierced the shield and gone through to embed itself in the heart of the cavalry leader. He did not move from where he landed on the turf.

Whilst all this had happened, Hartspell had taken care of his foe. He shot a bolt of blue light from his staff, blinding both the horse and rider as they bore down upon him. The former reared and the latter collapsed onto the earth holding his face. In addition, Meeshan and Spiny had dispatched the remainder of their opponents, and Angus trotted up nonchalantly to Séamus.

"Nice work, laddie," he said happily.

Díarmuid and his group had now defeated the other riders, those left standing having surrendered. Crannock had to be restrained when the surrender came; enraged believing Crellock's injury was more serious than it was. As it turned out, Crellock only had a leg wound that healed well with the aid of the Druid's healing spells once the arrow was removed. Hartspell also helped to curtail the pain and speed up the healing of others, with incantations and herbs; those of Díarmuid's party, of the prisoners and of the horses.

Of the original twenty-four in the cavalry unit that had attacked, only five were left alive. They were clearly shell-shocked at their defeat to an outnumbered and surprised foe, with but four fatalities of their own.

Díarmuid was furious and abashed at having lost four men though. On a practical level, it was a severe blow to a raiding party made up of only twenty. But on a personal level, it was a blow to him as a commander, responsible for the lives of those who followed him. Two of the casualties were shot in the original hail of arrows, Cian and Cet. Two more, Jarlath and Fionnuala, had died in the fierce fighting between Díarmuid's group of riders and the section of the enemy cavalry that they had charged.

The prisoners were made to sit for the moment in the centre of the group, once they had reassembled after injuries had been treated and mounts calmed and tethered. Díarmuid then turned angrily on Angus.

"Where was the warning!" he shouted at the scout.

"Ach, they were hidden and waiting. If I hadnae heard a horse I'd have walked straight into them and been kilt. As it was I took cover in time and managed to creep between two riders lying down in the heather with their beasties. That's all there was as far as I knew, then you came into view and up popped the rest. The question you should be asking yonsells is how they came to know ye were comin' at all?"

Angus gave his explanation matter-of-factly whilst cleaning his sword, clearly not holding himself in any way responsible for the surprise attack that had claimed two lives before the forces could be joined. Díarmuid breathed heavily and calmed himself as he listened to this, realising that there was merit in the explanation and that he could not really question the failure of the scout on this occasion. He was worried himself about the implications of this cavalry unit lying in wait for them, a concern that Angus had just put into words in front of one and all. He turned on the prisoners.

"Speak!" he shouted. "How came you to know of our arrival and why did you attack?"

The prisoners looked nervously at one another. Some flinched not knowing what rough treatment to expect at the hands of their captors, others looked down and said nothing. One at last spoke up.

"We saw – that is one of us saw on a patrol, from a distance, sir – a hideous creature and a mounted troop with him, tearing up the stakes on our borders. He noted your direction and a trap was set, seeing as it seemed the group were armed and ill disposed to the laws of Dragonsrealm, sir."

So spoke the prisoner, in fits and starts, eyes looking from one of his captors to another, proud but afraid. At the mention of 'a hideous creature', the two centaurs had to stop Spiny from running in at the poor man. Díarmuid was less than pleased with what he had heard also.

"Ill disposed to the laws of Dragonsrealm!" he roared. "It is you that does the tyrant's work! And you expect me to believe that you don't know who we are and that you weren't just sent here to delay us in liberating my kingdom?"

Díarmuid stepped forward as he spoke, pointing accusingly at the prisoners who flinched again. The same man answered once more, still proudly meeting Díarmuid's eye however, and he raised his voice also as he responded.

"We are keepers of the peace! We are not responsible for who rules here and many may wish for less harsh a regime, but that is not for us to decide. The giant protects his people. We have food in our bellies and no war on our land. Things were much worse before when the tyrant prince Eremil kept all in serfdom and took so much from the people, so that he might live in splendour whilst others starved!" He spoke passionately, and continued unabashed, despite the look of wrath spreading over Díarmuid's features.

"I have no idea who you are. You say this is your kingdom? You are but marauders from the lands of our enemies, who we saw only this morning destroying our border posts where traitors' heads look out to warn those who would assail us. May your heads adorn them soon! I—"

"Enough!" yelled Díarmuid. "I will listen to no more lies!"

Hartspell put a restraining hand upon Díarmuid's shoulder. "He speaks the truth, as he sees it," he said calmly. "I sense no deception."

"Lies," said Díarmuid again, more quietly to himself.

"Shall I question him more closely for you?" asked Angus, stepping forward, with an unfriendly glance at the captive who had spoken. The soldier closed his eyes and turned his head away, swallowing in fear, but said nothing.

"No," said Díarmuid, gently but firmly. Then more loudly, he spoke, facing the soldier who had accused him, so that all could hear.

"Understand; I am no torturer or tyrant like the giant Lokil. All men will be treated fairly whatever cause they follow." He faced his own followers now and indicated the prisoners with a sweep of his hands.

"For these men have been deceived," he continued. "But I will bring order and compassion back to Dragonsrealm, and rule as my brother Eremil did before me. For there were no wars and there was no tyranny before the giant came. People live in ignorance and fear, and we will put a stop to it. The prisoners can be released, without their mounts or weapons, when we continue tomorrow. The news of our arrival will only be behind us and they will not be able to spread it ahead of us."

He paused before adding finally, in a more sombre tone, "Now we will bury the dead. Then we will make camp. Meeshan will order the watches for me."

Then he walked away.

Chapter 13

The Blemmyai

Díarmuid stood on his own, with his back to the others, deep in contemplation of what had taken place and what he had heard. Meeshan carried out his commands efficiently and ordered the watches for the night. The prisoners spoke to each other in hushed whispers, not knowing what to believe; sometimes arguing over who Díarmuid really was and what the giant was really like. Sometimes talking anxiously about if their release would actually take place or if they should find their throats cut in the night. Needless to say, they did not get much sleep that night.

Séamus found it hard to sleep too. He had killed a man in the ambush. Díarmuid had been full of praise when he was given all the details of the fight. Séamus did not feel pleased though. He knew he had had no choice and did not feel guilty about it, but this was not the sort of adventure he wanted to be in. Comrades had been killed, and he had been forced to kill an enemy. Such skirmishes are all very well and good in stories or history books, but to be in one, where there was bloodshed and maiming and your life could be taken at any moment, that was not something that Séamus would wish on anybody.

He did not understand how Meeshan, Angus, Spiny and many of the others, Díarmuid even, saw it as a fact of life, even as a career. He did not understand either how he had been so focused and powerful in the combat itself, flinging the dagger with such force and accuracy with his wrong hand. And the leather strap where his watch had been had lit up as if some power were surging through him.

"You are troubled, Séamus?" asked Hartspell who had moved over to sit besides him. "Try and get some sleep."

"That fight. I don't know how I behaved the way I did. And the killing. I'm just not used to it," said Séamus sadly. He was looking down, subconsciously rubbing the leather strap on his left wrist with his right hand as he spoke.

"It is your gift here, Séamus," said the Druid.

"You have a military mind we noted earlier, a clearness of vision that did not desert you in the heart of the action. Some strength and skill also in that left arm of yours eh? Perhaps aided by that talisman, hmm?" the Druid chuckled, indicating the wrist strap.

"Or perhaps the power is in you and it merely reacts to it? Who can say? You are a reluctant warrior, and that is good. The best ones are."

The Druid got up then and moved to another part of the camp to talk to another of the night's insomniacs, Spiny, who found all the daylight travelling hard going. He would have much preferred to be awake and moving at night time.

In the morning, to the surprise of the prisoners, they were released and shepherded behind the party and told to walk towards the border for the duration of that day. This was the opposite direction to that which Díarmuid's group would take. As they departed, they looked nervously over their shoulders every now and again as if they thought they would be hunted down for sport after a certain distance, and when they got to be nearly out of sight at the brow of a small rise in the terrain, they broke into a run and disappeared from view.

Hartspell approached the laughing Díarmuid who was in much better spirits this morning, holding the shield of the cavalry leader who had been killed by Séamus.

"There is some strange power that I sense in this device," said the Druid, indicating the wolf motif that was common to all the shields. The only difference to this shield was a black stripe that crossed through where the wolf's eyes were.

As Díarmuid looked, suddenly the eyes of the wolf-picture moved to focus on him. Hartspell dropped the shield as if it was hot, and it landed on the ground, the wolf's face looking up at them. Díarmuid stepped back and put his hand on the hilt of his sword. Séamus gasped as the wolf's jaw now began to move. A feral, growling voice emitted from the shield.

"Go back," it said.

The shield glowed red, then white. The wolf's picture disintegrated into a vile green smoke as the heat increased, and was soon effaced from the shield, leaving it plain and charred. A mocking laughter seemed to trail away as the wolf's image vanished. No one spoke for a while; all eyes were fixed on the shield from whence the unnatural voice had assailed them.

"This Wolfspell is very powerful," said Hartspell at last.

"And he knows we are coming," said Meeshan. "What do we do now?" she asked straightforwardly, looking at Díarmuid as she spoke.

"We go on," he replied. "With all haste."

Without more ado, the party decamped and set out once more, Angus jogging up ahead, bewilderingly quickly, disappearing from sight as he resumed his scouting duties. They moved onwards at a great pace through the low foothills of Dragonsrealm throughout the morning and stopped for a brief break in the early afternoon so that the party and the horses could be refreshed.

Angus was recalled as Spiny had stated in conversation with Díarmuid in the course of the morning that the scout made the finest porridge he had ever tasted. "As good as The Dagda's," he said. As porridge was a quick meal to make when a Druid could provide the heat, this was to be their main repast before moving on.

Díarmuid sat down next to Séamus as they began to tuck in to a portion of Angus's fast food service. It was not like the porridge that you or I would be used to, but more like the porridge of old, with meats and herbs combined with the oats. It was warm, filling and delicious and it lifted everyone's spirits as if they were charmed by magic.

"Did Spiny tell you what his real name was?" asked Séamus, relaxing as he sat back and spooned a large helping of porridge into his mouth.

"No," replied Díarmuid, smiling and lowering his spoon.

"He talked about Angus and other friends more than himself. When I asked his name, he said it was difficult to translate from animal talk, so we should be content with what we knew."

Díarmuid chuckled then. "Which means it probably translates to Brushhead of Spikeybottom or something like that!"

Séamus laughed along with Díarmuid; it was good to share a joke again after the events of the previous day.

But his joviality was short lived. Suddenly the two of them found themselves dangling in the air, a huge paw holding each of them above ground by the throat. An angry voice shouted, "Having some fun at old Spiny's expense are you?"

A hairy face turned from one of them to the other resting a look on Díarmuid as he continued.

"Perhaps you need to learn some manners, prince and all you may be?"

"Cease! Cease!" yelled Hartspell, coming over to the scene as quickly as he could. "This is no way to carry on!"

"Save yon breath for cooling the porridge, my friend," added Angus trotting over, looking unusually anxious, knowing how powerful his friend's claws could be.

"A wee bit of a joke is nothing to you. The man ye're throttling there is the rightful ruler of them woods of yours. And wasnae he saying just before how invaluable ye were in the thick of that fight?"

The Druid seemed poised for action as the hedgehog struggled to master his temper. Addressing Angus, as if to make it plain that it was his words rather than the Druid's unspoken threat that counted, Spiny lowered his two companions and shuffled away growling after him.

"Just making my point, that's all. A bit of respect isn't too much to ask for."

Séamus and Díarmuid rubbed their hands around their throats and coughed to clear them now that their feet were returned to terra firma.

Díarmuid was in an awkward position. He immediately had to consider what, if any, action he could take. As leader of the party he needed to reprimand Spiny and reassert his authority. But he needed to do this without creating another incident and damaging morale, a difficult task with an acerbic hedgehog. He was interrupted however, before he could think, let alone do anything. Two of the men, who had been keeping watch on the perimeter of the camp whilst the others took their meal, came running in towards him.

"There's dozens of creatures," said the front-runner of the two, Donall.

"Coming straight towards the camp," added Cormac behind him.

Díarmuid did not need to give the order. The whole camp made ready, mounted their horses, where applicable, and prepared weapons.

"More soldiers?" asked Díarmuid.

"No. They have no uniform," said Cormac, looking sidelong at Donall.

"No heads either," added Donall. "It's the Blemmyai."

At that point a large number of figures came into view of the camp. They were all on foot, all between five and five and a half foot in height, with a tan-coloured skin and tufts of brownish hair. They all had dark trews on but their large feet were bare, as were their torsos. This was because, as Donall had correctly pointed out, they had no heads. Or rather, their heads were in their chests, so that their tufted crowns only just appeared above the line of their shoulders.

They held longbows with a quiver of arrows awkwardly fixed across from their shoulders to their midriff so that the strap nestled against their features in their chests. Small swords were also visible attached to the top of their trews by a scabbard. The Blemmyai had lived in peace within Dragonsrealm and other kingdoms during Eremil's time, but they kept very much to themselves and were viewed with suspicion.

Before Díarmuid could stop him, Crellock had raised his bow on seeing the creatures approach holding their long bows, even though they were initially set so that the arrows were directed groundwards. Instantly, one of the Blemmyai raised a bow and shot down the centaur, piercing the same leg that was injured during the previous combat.

"Not again!" groaned Crellock as he hit the ground, attempting to remove the arrow.

At this, Crannock and Spiny got ready to charge and the others now held their weapons poised.

"Hold your fire!" yelled Díarmuid, stalling any response.

The two groups eyed each other for a moment. It was Díarmuid who spoke first, deciding he needed to seize the initiative to prove to his own party the quality of his leadership, especially after the recent assault by Spiny.

"Do you come so arrayed against us for battle?" he asked defiantly, despite the large numerical advantage of the creatures. "If so, prepare for a fierce contest, else depart and leave us to our business."

One of the creatures stepped out from amongst the others. He was one of the taller of the Blemmyai present and had stripes of red dye through his tufted hair.

"I was going to ask the same question," spoke the creature clearly, in a slightly high-pitched voice.

Again Séamus recognised that the creature was speaking its own language, but that his mind adjusted the sounds to hear the meaning of the communication without any effort.

"And seeing as this is our territory," he continued, waving his arm about him to indicate the land on which they stood, "although the cursed giant may think otherwise, I would say it was for you to explain yourselves."

So saying he folded his arms below his chest and face and waited. The other Blemmyai stood poised in an arc in front of Díarmuid and his men.

Séamus counted fifty of them, at least.

Chapter 14

A Night Attack

Díarmuid decided to take a chance. They were outnumbered and the Blemmyai were excellent archers, especially at such a range as this, less than one hundred yards. The leading Blemmyai, or their spokesman, had stated that he had no love for Lokil at least. This was the opening Díarmuid needed to speak boldly and yet still bring his diplomacy to bear and prevent bloodshed.

"I am Díarmuid, brother to Eremil. So I too may lay claim to this land as the cursed giant does. I come to reclaim it. If you will not help, at least do not hinder us. You may depart as I say, and leave us to our business."

He too now folded his arms and waited. Meeshan nodded in approval of his proud stance and Angus grinned broadly. Spiny was still chomping at the bit as they say, and a sidelong look from the Druid as he tended Crellock was all that held him back.

Séamus felt that mixture of fear and calmness come over him that he had experienced in the previous encounter with the soldiers. He found himself thinking of the best place to break the ranks of the Blemmyai to cause maximum confusion should they need to charge their lines and face their bows.

The eyes of the leading Blemmyai narrowed for a moment, affronted by the bold response, yet thoughtful of its content. He looked either side of him in a way that led to the other Blemmyai lowering their bows, once more pointing them at the ground. He faced Díarmuid again.

"I am Chouda of the Blemmyai. Our warrens are near here and extend beneath your feet. We could easily surround you, but I have no wish to hinder your cause. We should speak," he said.

Díarmuid did not move. "I am in haste," he replied.

"Nevertheless we should speak. You said 'if you will not help'. Well perhaps we will help. Your force is not large and may need it. The giant is our enemy; his forces harry us and send smoke into our warrens because we do not serve him. But I would know first before I offer help, to whom it is that I offer it. What plans has he for the Blemmyai?" He stepped forward as he spoke, one of his men accompanying him, as if the matter were settled.

Díarmuid thought a moment about challenging this assertion, but decided that the time spent negotiating with the Blemmyai may prove invaluable. He may double the size of his raiding party, or even do better if all of the Blemmyai present were available to him. It was also an opportunity to create some trust with a people who would be tenants on his land and about whom he, and his brother before him, had known very little.

"I will speak with you as you wish," he answered, stepping forwards himself.

"In the middle here where all can plainly see us."

Chouda nodded as if that was in his mind also. Hartspell gave Díarmuid a look of confidence and approval as he went alone to parley with Chouda and his companion between the two arrayed forces.

There was an uneasy silence on both sides of the conference as Díarmuid and the two Blemmyai talked and talked, for half an hour at least, before each returned to his own group. The conversation had been usually calm and there was never a sense of animosity, but at times the debate between them had seemed animated. However, an understanding had clearly been reached.

Díarmuid addressed his men whilst Chouda seemed to be organising his.

"The Blemmyai have agreed to send with us fifteen warriors. Chouda and his general Sourbal who spoke with me hither will be amongst them. They are fleet of foot and will have no difficulty keeping pace with us on horseback. Sourbal will scout ahead with Angus."

Díarmuid mounted his horse in an assured manner and no one questioned his decision nor asked what guarantees he had given the Blemmyai in return for their contribution. His leadership, if it had been in doubt, was unquestionable now.

The band that set off for Dragonshill Mountain to confront Lokil in the rath of the prince was now far more considerable. The plan to confront Lokil as swiftly as they could before word was spread of their incursion, and before a large defence could be assembled, was still thought to be achievable. The Blemmyai had confirmed that no word of Díarmuid's presence had reached them.

Chouda's general and scout trotted up alongside Angus.

"I'll stick to the left ahead if ye'll keep right," said Angus in a neutral tone to the Blemmyai. He was pleased to have the help of another scout so that he would not have such a large area to be patrolling and watching ahead of the party. His vanity was such though that he fancied he did not need any help and that the new addition would not do half as good a job as he could himself.

Sourbal signalled his assent with a slight bow and a blink of the eyes. "I will do as you suggest," he said, "though I don't mind saying that I told Chouda I've got a bad feeling about all this."

Grimly Sourbal retired to his position and Angus did the same, not cheered by the creature's lack of confidence. Both scouts were soon lost to sight in rocks, heather, gorse and grass.

Soon the land started to rise more steeply. The green fields of the rolling hills and valleys disappeared and the route became more cumbersome. Moorland and springy turf were the norm with large outcrops of stone appearing more regularly to limit the options of travelling more than one or two abreast. On one side or another intermittently there appeared bog cotton and everyone did their best to stay on the rough track as Díarmuid warned that the bogs were always changing here and you could not be sure where it was safe to step. By nightfall, they came to the beginning of a mountainous region and the base of a long pass, the tail of Dragonshill Mountain.

This was Dragonshill Ridge. The track from here on could only take one at a time on horseback and there was little a scout ahead could do other than run into trouble before everyone else did, if there was trouble to be found. If they were to walk non-stop through the night, by dawn some five hours hence they may be in view of Dragonshill Fort.

Spiny and a few others were for continuing through the night for the benefits of speed and surprise. Hartspell and Díarmuid were more of the opinion that they should camp now and move off at dawn as it would be treacherous to follow the ridge path at night, and also because most needed the rest. After his success earlier in the day in winning over the Blemmyai, everyone was content enough to agree to Díarmuid's strategy, although Spiny was heard to moan to Angus that there was light enough by the moon.

Sentries were posted a little up the pass ahead of them and around the camp behind them, and a small campfire was lit in a hollow to conceal the flames. Hartspell examined Crellock's second injury and pronounced it healed and no longer in need of the bandage. The centaur had struggled to keep up at the back of the party with his brother in the afternoon despite the attentions of the Druid, as even with magical healing to speed the process, wounds and pains do not disappear completely for many an hour.

It was about the middle of that short night, when it was at its darkest and the time that the Blemmyai were about to take over watch duties, that an unexpected attack came from above. Three ugly winged hags known as Harpies descended upon the party with claws and teeth and in a moment there was mayhem in the camp. It had been fortunate though that they had struck when the watch was changing and many were up and about, otherwise things may have been much worse.

As it was, Díarmuid, who had been awake in the earlier watch, was able to reach one hag with his greatsword and cut her in two. A Blemmyai had wounded another that attacked it with an upward thrust of a shortsword, and when it looked as if this would not be enough to save him, Séamus had managed also to stab it in the leg with his dagger. Again, the leather strap on his left wrist glowed briefly and the Harpy screamed in pain and released its grip on the Blemmyai. It then flew away bleeding heavily from its two wounds and the third Harpy, left alone, was easily driven off by sheer numbers before she was able to carry off one of her victims to feed.

The Harpies had done plenty of damage though. They had hit the Blemmyai hard and with surprise as they had taken up their positions for the watch. Two Blemmyai were dead, two more Blemmyai and two of the men from the village injured in the ensuing melee.

Most did not sleep now for the remainder of the night. Díarmuid was not worried about the Harpies reporting their presence, as they are more like animals in their nature and would have been independent of Lokil or Wolfspell. He suspected though that they might have been brought here to guard the mountain pass by one or other of them.

"To think that these creatures should be allowed to roam once more in our mountains," Díarmuid spat between clenched teeth quietly to himself.

"The giant and his Druid will pay dearly for this."

Hartspell had treated the two men who had been injured, Niall and Dafydd, but they were still feverish as the Harpy is a diseased and poisonous being. They could not go on at daybreak and remained with two more of the Blemmyai to protect them and to return the bodies of their dead to their warren. It was the two injured Blemmyai who undertook this task, although they seemed impervious to the effect of the Harpies' poison.

As they departed, Séamus secretly examined a small scratch on his left hand near his leather strap. The Harpy had caught him slightly with a claw. The wound had healed leaving a small scar, but Séamus felt a little light-headed, not feverish like the other men, but he knew he had been affected. He feared saying anything lest he should be left behind. He knew he had to continue with this adventure wherever it took him, or he may not get the chance to get home. He must stay in with Hartspell and Díarmuid. He mounted Misty and prepared to continue as if nothing were wrong.

The party now moved up along the pass. Sourbal and Angus were about fifty yards ahead of the rest on the winding trail. They did their best to remain in cover of the boulders and small trees and bushes that grew on the mountainside near the ridge, but were for long periods out of cover. For the most part they were out of sight of the main group also, as the path seldom remained straight for a stretch of fifty yards or more. It still rose and the air became colder. Meeshan and Spiny guarded the rear of the group, taking turns to walk backwards and ensure there was nothing to be concerned about behind them. Most often it was Meeshan who did this, as it is not easy for a seven-foot long hedgehog to move backwards uphill on a ridge not much wider than himself.

Angus and Sourbal carried on slowly and methodically. They came to a particularly steep rise where they could see that the path descended out of view for a while once they should reach the top of this section of track. Away to their right they could see it skirting around the middle of another mountain in the range, but as yet they could not see the layout of the path that must dip down to this level over the peak ahead of them. Because of this, they were both walking more cautiously when they heard the strange and blood-curdling scream, like a squawk of a large and agonised bird.

Sourbal looked at Angus. "I've a really bad feeling about this," he said, as he drew his sword. He crawled silently up to look over the top of the rise at what lay ahead of them on the path below. Angus followed him drawing his claymore and signalling for the party behind to halt. They had already done so, for they too had heard the terrifying scream.

Chapter 15

The Cockatrice

Sourbal peeped over the top of the rise where the path dipped, then retreated very suddenly indeed.

"Cockatrice!" he hissed. "He didn't see me."

"You don't say," said Angus sarcastically eyeing his companion humorously.

Now it was a little unfair of Angus to be so flippant. The stare of a Cockatrice can turn you to stone, but only if it decides to attack and if it gets a reasonable look at you. When it is not alarmed, or not hungry, it may decide to look at you without aggression and then no harm will befall you. Unfortunately, it is a jumpy bird (or serpent, depending on your viewpoint) and usually feels threatened by everything and is always happy to turn any living creature to stone for a snack later, even if it is not hungry at the time. Presumably when it breaks up the statue of the creature it has petrified and eats a chunk, that stone will return to a digestible form of flesh within its gizzard. Otherwise, if it could digest rock, the creature could just eat ordinary stones, one would have thought.

Perhaps it can, and it just has a bit of an attitude problem. This is common to all forms of Basilisk, and a Cockatrice is no exception. It has a serpent's body but the head, tail and feet of a cockerel and a very unpleasant cockcrow to go with it. You may have heard the story of Medusa, the Gorgon killed by Perseus, with writhing serpents on her head. They too were a form of Basilisk that could turn living flesh to stone with a good hard stare.

Hartspell referred to the Cockatrice as one of "Balor's children". Séamus knew the story of Balor, the wicked leader of the Fomorians, and his evil eye. It took ten men to lift the heavy lid of the eye and all whom his glance fell upon would be killed. But Lugh of the Tuatha De Danaan, who was also Balor's grandson, killed him with a slingshot through the eye when Balor attempted to open it at the Battle of Moytura, after Lugh had taunted him. The Tuatha De Danaan were then victorious and Lugh became their king, Nuada having previously been slain by Balor in the battle. According to Hartspell, in the brief time he had to explain his reference, the eye of Balor as he lay dying alighted on a nest of serpents. These were transformed rather than killed by the dying glance, and the Druids could not catch and kill them all. Some of these now magical creatures fled to the Otherworld to become the progenitors of all types of Basilisk.

As the party quietly discussed what to do about the Cockatrice patrolling the path over the hill and below them, Séamus remembered the story of Perseus also. He addressed Hartspell.

"Do you have a mirror? We could maybe hold it up over the hill there and see where it is and what it is doing. When its back is turned someone could hop up and take a shot at it."

"Excellent idea, excellent," said Hartspell. "Didn't I say he thought very clearly on such matters?"

Díarmuid nodded approvingly.

"Now," continued the Druid, "I don't have a mirror, but the bird might spot it held over the top there anyway. The best thing is for a vision spell, I don't know why I didn't think of it before, but you put it in my mind with your idea, Séamus."

The Druid now borrowed Díarmuid's shield and placed its outside down on the ground so the inside of it appeared like a large bowl in front of him. He mumbled a couple of words;

Séamus noticed he never could tell what the Druid was saying when he did this unlike his understanding of everyone else's languages. An image of the path beyond the hill could now be seen in the shield, dipping down and then levelling out to skirt around the next mountain as Sourbal had reported. The Cockatrice could now be seen, near the point where the path rose on the other side of the hill, pausing as if to decide whether it would carry on and climb up. Slowly, it could then be seen beginning the ascent, looking from left to right as it proceeded in much the same way as a hen or a cockerel would do when it walks.

"I don't think it's going to turn its back," said Hartspell, "It must have heard something and it's coming towards us. Someone is going to have to take a chance and shoot it when it's looking away to our right."

"It takes time to aim a bow," said Chouda at this. "I've no doubt that one of my people, or one of your warriors," he added looking at Díarmuid, "would get a hit in and kill it, but not before it got a good look at the marksman and petrified a part of him."

"Yet it must be attempted," said Meeshan stepping forward, as if to volunteer.

Then Séamus heard himself saying quietly, "I'll do it."

All eyes turned on him quizzically.

"With my dagger," said Séamus, a little embarrassed now and surprised at what he had just suggested. It was as if a warrior personality within him, the one that had appeared with such clarity in this world, had seen the solution and Séamus could not deny him.

"It will take no time to aim like a bow, and I'm confident I can hit anything within range if I can see it. I don't know how, but I can. I'll get up quickly on your word, Hartspell, when it's looking away to the right, throw, and be down again before it gets a look."

All were quiet for a moment.

"There is still a great risk, Séamus," said the Druid at last, frowning.

"You do not have to do this, though I think it is the best solution," added Díarmuid.

Séamus breathed deeply. "I *will* do it," he said.

"Then quickly," said Hartspell decisively. "Get to the top there and await my word. The Cockatrice is nearly half way up."

Séamus got to the top of the path before it levelled out and dropped away again. He lay flat, waiting for the word to act, afraid and yet calm, thinking of the mythological monster over the rim of the hill.

"Now!" hissed Hartspell suddenly, as loudly as he dared for fear of alerting the nearby creature.

Instantly Séamus leaped up, his left arm already drawn back ready to throw. The Cockatrice was looking away to the right down the mountainside, below and to the right of Séamus, still over one hundred yards away. Yet Séamus's aim was still true. He saw the dagger fly at speed, as if directed by a laser, straight into the chest of the serpent's body below the head of the bird. He felt the surge of power in his wrist again and the light blazed on the sundial pattern on his leather strap below his wrist.

But as soon as he had released the dagger, Séamus had been aware that the creature was turning towards the sudden movement above it. Instinctively, whilst diving for cover again, he had raised his right arm in front of his head. It seemed like no time had passed in the moment before the dying squawk of the Cockatrice was heard, but Séamus was aware that he had been attacked.

A sharp pain, like a bee's sting, followed by a severe tingling sensation spread throughout his lower right arm. Séamus examined the area from where he lay. Between his hand and his elbow, his arm looked grey and rigid. It felt painfully heavy. It had been turned to stone by the dying glance of the Cockatrice.

A look of concern filled the faces of Séamus's comrades as they gathered around him. They had raced up to congratulate him having seen the death of the monster in Hartspell's shield-mirror. Their eyes now sought out the Druid's verdict anxiously as Hartspell softly lifted and felt Séamus's injured arm.

"Can you move your fingers at all?" asked the Druid.

Séamus concentrated. His fingers on his right hand twitched a little, his human hand looking alien on the end of the statue's arm.

"That is good," said Hartspell. "It cannot be completely transformed, there is still an internal connection between the upper arm and the hand, if but a small one. I can do nothing for him here to alleviate the magic however, not without special herbs from my garden. You must keep that arm in a sling Séamus and ensure that no harm comes to it. It will chip and crack very easily and when I restore your arm, we don't want bits missing."

As he spoke, the Druid had produced from inside his cloak a bandage, with which he expertly made and applied the sling. Díarmuid looked downcast and uncomfortable at the sight of Séamus so damaged, having promised that no harm would come to him and that he would get home safely. Séamus caught his eye.

"I'm alright," he said. "It's heavy, but the sling supports it, and I can still feel my hand."

"You are a remarkable lad," said Díarmuid proudly, "that you should think to comfort me at this time."

"Come on," he added to the rest of the party now. "Let's get going. The Cockatrice was left out here to guard this path, someone may have heard its final scream and interpreted it as an attack. But we may be lucky. The rath is but a couple of hours away now and we must proceed swiftly. No scouts. I will lead."

Díarmuid led his horse over the rise and down the path on the other side whilst the rest of the group sorted out the order in which they should follow. Hartspell moved up to accompany Díarmuid, the path was wide enough again for two to walk side by side. After them and their mounts came Chouda and Meeshan, Séamus after that with Emer, the other men, women and Blemmyai intermixed in the ranks behind them. At the end of the party were the two Centaurs, then Spiny on his own, and finally Angus and Sourbal together, now protecting the rear.

The going was hard although the track widened a little and in places the men could go on horseback again. Séamus sweated and at times felt a little dizzy. His right arm felt heavy, and the scar on his left hand now throbbed making his heartbeat seem loud in his ears. He thought about telling the Druid about the scar as he surely could not be left behind now, but he decided against it. Hartspell had not been able to completely cure the other men who the Harpies had wounded anyway, and Díarmuid had enough to worry about as he finally approached his home after centuries away. A home occupied by an unfriendly giant.

The track had descended to pass around the base of the mountain as they had seen from the height previously, but they were still very high up and the air was thin. Once around that section, the path twisted to the left and it began to rise again between two more peaks.

Díarmuid stopped momentarily and looked around at the troop behind him.

"Once we are at the top of this gully," he said, "we will gaze upon my home, and my fortress, Dragonshill Rath. Prepare yourselves."

He spurred on his horse and rode up now ahead of Hartspell, eager for a view of his home, or perhaps eager for the confrontation that he knew must come with Lokil the giant. Hartspell did his best to keep pace with him and the others now followed with drawn swords.

Chapter 16

A Note on the Door

Dragonshill Rath was a simple affair. It had a square earthwork base, roughly fifty metres each side, faced with stone, and it stood tall overlooking the valleys below it and the mountains above it. It had three storeys, not counting the roof, which could also be patrolled and had guardrooms in the tops of the turrets at each corner. The upper two levels were constructed entirely of thick timber; the lower storey was fashioned out of local stone. Below ground were cellars and prison cells. The rath sat on a flat top of the furthest mountain in the range, the Dragon's Head, with steep cliffs beyond it and to the sides of it. These cliffs contained ridges that could be viewed as features, perhaps ears, a nose, a mouth and teeth, of the animal after which the mountain was named.

This mountain was not the highest of the range, and Díarmuid gazed down upon it from the track a mile away on a high ridge of the neighbouring summit. It was secure though; the only access not beset by cliffs was to the front where a wide track descended in open ground so all who approached were visible. This track split a few hundred yards from the fort, one going down the mountain to the fields and valleys and villages below, the other continuing up to the next mountain and onwards across the range which Díarmuid's party had just traversed.

Díarmuid noticed that the drawbridge was down, but the moat looked empty, no more than a dry ditch. The outer wall, an extra defence beyond the moat, was damaged and the gates that had stood within that wall where the track steered towards the drawbridge and the entrance to the fort were gone. This was thirty yards from the fort, a perfect distance for throwing stones, spears or javelins at any foe that broke through that point.

There was no sign of any movement, no obvious sentries, and there was an eerie silence. Normally any sound, even a small cough, from Dragonshill Rath would have travelled up to the ridge on which Díarmuid stood, discernible and clear.

"We will all go down to the outer wall," said Díarmuid, turning to the raiding party behind him. "The place looks deserted, and even if it were not, there is no need for stealth from hereon in. We cannot approach unobserved."

"Perhaps it is a trap?" asked Chouda, looking concerned. "Why would the fort be empty?"

"The rooms are too small for the giant?" offered Hartspell.

"But why are there no soldiers anyway?" asked Séamus.

"Out on other business. Probably attacking my wood!" grumbled Spiny, looking down to the right where a forest could be seen in the distance on low hills beyond the villages. "Who cares!" he continued. "We came to attack the fort. Let's attack now and ask questions later!"

Díarmuid smiled. "Indeed, that is why we are here. But first, assuming we are unmolested, we will stop at the outer wall and see what we will see before continuing further."

At this the party readied themselves for the final journey down to the rath. Some were tense, some eager, all brandished their weapons and looked about themselves fully alert for any ambush. Séamus felt a little less dizzy than earlier in the day, but he knew he was running a temperature and he was grateful that he was not burdened with heavy armour like Meeshan at his side. He needed to keep moving forward with the adventure. He wanted to reach the conclusion as soon as he could, so that, hopefully, Hartspell and Díarmuid would be free to find the path to his home where he would meet Granddad again in the Tavern.

"I've got a bad feeling about this," said Sourbal at the back of the party.

"Shut up," said Angus besides him. "You have a bad feeling about everything!"

"I'm usually right though," replied the Blemmyai.

"Ach, we'll be grand," said Angus smiling again now, "so long as we keep our heads."

Sourbal frowned back at him and made no comment, not knowing whether the pun was intentional or not, but strongly suspecting that it was.

The two walked on again at the back of the party, like all those before them, in complete silence.

They got to the outer wall without incident. The wall was badly damaged around the area where the gates used to be, and the pathway passed through the gaping hole to meet with the drawbridge over the now drained moat. Hartspell had suggested that Díarmuid remain at the wall at first whilst he approached the fort itself, in case a magic defence was in place. Díarmuid reluctantly agreed not to risk himself at this point, and the Druid went forward selecting Spiny, Chouda and Sourbal for protection, thinking that they would be more impervious to a magic attack than any of the others.

Cautiously, the four crossed the drawbridge to the large oak-panelled doors, similar to those at Hartspell's own home, but more rectangular. There was still no sound and nobody assailed them as they came right beneath the walls of the rath. It was then that a small patch of white on the doors, which had caught Hartspell's attention as he had crossed the drawbridge, could be identified. Lokil had left a note.

Hartspell could sense no charm set to entrap the reader, so he carefully reached up above his head to take the note down – the giant had clearly misjudged the height of likely visitors, although he had put it quite low by his own standards. It read, roughly translated, as follows:

This castle is solely the residence of Lokil the Giant,
Lord of the Ice Mountain Golath,
Most revered King in the land called Dragonsrealm.
Petitions for mercy will only be heard by appointment.
Should the appointment be too late for clemency,
My good wishes for you in your next life,
Try not to get into any more trouble then.
If you are reading this note, then I am not here.
Go away now.
If you are still here when I return,
Or if you have entered my castle,
You will be killed.
Probably slowly – to set an example.

Kind Regards,

Lokil.

Hartspell returned over the drawbridge to show the note to
Díarmuid. Díarmuid was furious at the title the giant had
given himself; no one had ever called themselves a king in
Dragonsrealm before. The ruler took the title of Prince, as the
king was said to be the sleeping dragon on which the realm
resided.

He decided that they would enter the rath and await the
giant's return, surprising him and putting an end to his reign
and his life.

Lokil was clearly too sure of his position to think that he
could live by himself up here with nobody daring to strike at
him and his tyranny.

Díarmuid determined to go into the castle at once, but
Meeshan expressed the view that they should still be cautious
in case the note was a deception and servants were lying in
wait inside, loyal to their master. Again Díarmuid was
persuaded to hold back for the moment and not to risk a
premature end to his campaign.

After a short discussion with Meeshan, Spiny stood on his back paws and threw her straight up in the air from the base of the doors so that she went over the top of them and onwards to a small rampart six feet above the doorway. She grabbed at the rail on the rampart as she reached it and cat-like sprang over the edge to land on her feet, crouched down with sword drawn instantly, ready for action. She was, for the moment, on her own. She stood up and looked over the top of the rampart and shouted down to Díarmuid, "Which way to the doors?"

"Right or left to one of the towers," answered Díarmuid, "then down one flight of steps to ground level – you'll enter into the main hall and see the doors at the centre."

With a nod of acknowledgment, Meeshan was on her way.

A minute later, though it felt like ten to Díarmuid, the sound of bolts being drawn behind the door could be heard. Everybody tensed and stood with weapons ready as the doors swung open.

Meeshan stood there with one hand on her hip and waved them in ceremoniously with her other arm.

"Nobody home," she said.

After a couple of hours had gone by, the party ascertained that this was indeed true by carrying out a thorough search of all the levels, above and below ground, of Dragonshill Rath. The horses had been tethered at the rear of the fort, out of sight of any of the approaches, and defences were prepared for the giant's return. The centaurs stayed with the horses to guard them and to comfort them, so that they would not whinny in fear and give away their presence should they hear or smell an enemy approach.

Many of the men and the Blemmyai now armed themselves with large pikes found in the armoury, so that they would have a better chance of damaging the giant should they find themselves in close proximity to him. Díarmuid had satisfied himself that the treasury and the armoury were pretty much unmolested, if anything the giant had added extra weapons and more treasures to the collections, though who had suffered in losing these artefacts Díarmuid did not like to think.

It was the golden harp on the first floor that got the most attention however. Much of the furniture had been smashed and not replaced with anything, presumably too small for the giant and in his way as he tried to move his massive frame inside the rath. The harp was another new addition; beautiful and dazzling, residing near a large table, one of the few surviving pieces of furniture, presumably something that the giant could use. There were numerous jars of varying size on the table near the harp, some containing potions and others tablets, but none of the jars were labelled.

Hartspell and Séamus stood by the table, the former looking at the multitude of bottles and jars, the latter transfixed by the beauty of the harp.

"I wonder," said the Druid. "The giant took a chance bringing a Cockatrice to guard the path over the mountain. Did he have an immunity to its spell, or is there a potion here that made him resist an attack?"

Séamus turned his attention to Hartspell now.

"Do you mean something here could cure my arm?" he asked hopefully.

"Impossible to tell," shrugged the Druid. "It may be there is something, but it may have to be taken before you met the Cockatrice to stop the effects in the first place. Or it may be that it would only work on a giant. Or it may be that the giant had some other magic to protect him. Or it may—"

"I get the picture," interrupted Séamus disappointedly. "There's no way you can tell."

"Sorry, Séamus, I—" but this time another voice interrupted the Druid. It was musical and beautiful, one voice, but like a gentle choir of angels, soft, clear and pure.

"The yellow bottle will prevent and heal any evil done by any type of Basilisk. Sip only a small drop for your damaged arm, else it will be too powerful and you will sleep, perhaps never to wake."

It was unmistakeable. The strings on the harp had moved, as if plucked by invisible hands, as the voice spoke.

Hartspell said nothing but took a step backwards as if presented with a threat. "Wh-Who are you?" stuttered Séamus, equally astonished.

"I am Caitlín, spirit of a Dryad, daughter of a Willow tree. The giant killed my tree and forced craftsmen to make this instrument, encased with gold. With his magic and the aid of his Druid I was trapped within this harp for his entertainment. I play for my own joy though, not for him. He knows not that I speak. Nor that I hear."

The speech was melancholy yet still beautiful and the harp strings moved in a dizzying flurry as Caitlín spoke.

"The magic is strong," whispered Hartspell to Séamus, looking suspiciously at the harp. "I sense no malice or deception but I cannot be certain that it is not masked. I can cure your arm later. Do not take this risk."

"How long will it take for your herbs and your magic to heal me?" Séamus whispered back, though not so low and carefully as the Druid.

"A few weeks I suppose," answered Hartspell.

"And it may yet be a while before we head back to get the herbs? What if I go back to my own world without having it healed? Will the stone change back and will I be harmed?"

Hartspell inhaled deeply, and then sighed. "I do not know. I cannot imagine that you will be undamaged from such a venture."

Séamus nodded. "I know I can get back in theory whenever I choose, but I don't feel easy about staying here for a month to heal – anything could happen, even assuming everything goes okay with Díarmuid's plans. You sense no danger and the voice is so beautiful—"

"Perilously beautiful?" interrupted the Druid.

"I don't think so," said Séamus decisively. "The yellow bottle?" he said, lifting the cork stopper from the large yellow bottle to his left on the table. The harp just played a soft note of music as if in confirmation. Séamus decided to trust the harp-dryad and his instincts, and to take a sip of the potion.

Chapter 17

Lokil Returns

Séamus could not lift the bottle, small though it must have been for the giant; it was over a foot big, wide at the base, and nearly full with a heavy, sticky, clear liquid. Hartspell made no move to stop Séamus, but looked on with a frown of concern, no doubt readying spells to counter any treachery that might occur.

Séamus dipped a finger in the wide opening; enough to get a sticky drop of liquid from around the mouth of the bottle onto it.

He took a taste, grimaced momentarily at the bitterness and then closed his eyes in pain as a sudden jolt like an electric shock exploded over his petrified arm. Hartspell stood back in alarm as blue fire filigreed over the area of stone, holding his breath to determine the outcome.

In a moment, the blue flames disappeared. Séamus was left holding his right arm in his left hand, rubbing it because the tingling sensation had not stopped. But the arm was whole and was flesh again.

Hartspell bowed towards the harp.

"Thank you, Caitlín," he said.

"Yes. Th-thank you," repeated Séamus, smiling and in awe.

The harp played another few notes in pleasure, but said nothing, and then a new, distant, thumping noise suddenly assailed their ears. Séamus and Hartspell shared a glance, each to ascertain that they had both heard the same sound. There was no doubt a second later. From below, Angus's voice could be heard from the front rampart.

"Yon giant beastie. Here he comes!"

Everyone that could took up positions around the perimeter of the main hallway behind the front doors, which had been closed and bolted once more. Others lined the stairway and parapet above on the next floor, bows at the ready. About half of the men and the Blemmyai had left by a back entrance to circle around to the front in case of other arrivals and to block any retreat that the giant might attempt. Despite this, it still felt a little crowded and it was unlikely that all that remained would all be able to assist in fighting the giant in a meaningful way in such a confined space.

Angus reported that the giant was sporting a huge wooden club but otherwise seemed unarmed. However, he wore a massive shaggy tunic that could have concealed a number of items. They heard the footsteps stop in front of the door.

"The note!" hissed Hartspell. "We did not replace the note!"

Suddenly there was a booming voice.

"Who has taken my note? Does anyone dare to enter my home?"

Díarmuid bristled at this but remained still and quiet. Had he been on the outside of the rath, he would have gasped with amazement though as the doors that he was familiar with suddenly developed a broad wooden mouth. Nothing of this was evident from the inside of the doors, however, yet everyone heard the reply.

"The note was taken down by a visitor. He and his companions are inside."

Now, fortunately for Díarmuid and the others, the giant did not stop to ask the door how many of the companions there were. If he had he may well have thought better of what he did next.

In a rage, he yelled "Open!" and the bolts flew back, the doors shot open, and in ran Lokil the giant, brandishing his metal studded club, looking for the intruders.

Díarmuid calmly stepped out from his cover at the side of the hallway, behind one of the many pieces of smashed or overturned furniture.

"This is my home, Lokil, not yours," he announced. "I am Díarmuid, brother of Eremil who you have slain, rightful Prince of Dragonsrealm. There are too many here for you to fight. Lay down your weapon and ask forgiveness, then exile will be your doom only. Refuse, and we will show no mercy."

The giant stood aghast and immobile at this speech, staring in disbelief at the small warrior in front of him, the lost prince returned. A fear suddenly gripped the giant for the first time in its long existence, and for a moment everyone thought that he would acknowledge the truth of his position, disarm and withdraw from Dragonshill.

But then the rage returned. The giant's eyes narrowed and with a roar his response came. The club swung ferociously straight at Díarmuid.

Many things were instigated by this fatal act of the giant's.

Díarmuid leaped nimbly to the side, but the impact of the club sent masonry flying and shook the ground so that he then fell heavily, not far from the giant's huge feet. A flurry of arrows came from above as the Blemmyai revealed themselves, and the giant roared in pain, plucking two of the many that had hit their target out of his side with his free fist.

With the dust of the masonry thick in the air, the Blemmyai were unable to fire more arrows with certainty, especially as both Meeshan and Angus had rushed out to assist Díarmuid, the three of them now in close proximity to the giant. Angus dragged Díarmuid up and away as the giant prepared another swing of his club at the prince who would replace him.

Meeshan stood firmly in his way and blocked the blow with her shield, the blow sending her flying backwards several feet. Impossibly, she rolled upright, unhurt, the shield still intact, gritting her teeth. She was cornered this time however, as the giant advanced on her again, the new focus of his fury.

Séamus felt his new warrior-sense coming over him again. Meeshan could not withstand another such blow where she stood. She would be knocked back into the wall and even with her lightning-fast reactions, she would not be able to stay on her feet or retain her shield, assuming that it could take another such hit without buckling.

Shouting to distract Lokil, Séamus ran with a pike pointing downwards at the giant's feet. The giant turned sideways to see his new tiny opponent, and flicked his club out contemptuously to swat him away. Again, Séamus found he had skills he did not realise as he easily dodged right underneath the club then, swiftly and surely, raised the pike and thrust upwards, impaling the giant in his belly.

Lokil screamed in pain, but surprisingly quick himself, pulled the pike out with his left hand, leaving Séamus dangling on the end of it. Just in time, Séamus dropped off and rolled out of reach, as the giant reeled the weapon in and made a grab for him.

Before Lokil could then swipe at any of his foes again with his weapon, the Druid managed to focus his magic upon it. The club heated up and glowed red, forcing Lokil to drop it. Angus, Meeshan and Díarmuid and a couple of the Blemmyai stood around him now with drawn swords, but Lokil was now berserk and could not have stopped to surrender.

He had recognised magic being cast and his powers enabled him to locate and identify Hartspell, who stood near the bottom of the stairwell, as the perpetrator. He lunged towards him with a huge stride, ignoring the painful cuts to his legs by the swords of Angus and Chouda who were forced out of his way. Díarmuid had spotted his chance though, and reacted just in time.

He cut a rope that supported a huge, single chandelier that hung above the bottom of the stairwell, and the heavy iron rings and interlocking chains smashed down on top of Lokil. The largest of the rings had become attached to the giant's head like a circlet, as he struggled to try and gain his feet whilst covered in dust and blood, inches from the Druid. Hartspell moved backwards and up several steps on the stairs.

"Surrender now, while you still can, and swear allegiance to Prince Díarmuid," said Hartspell coolly.

The giant panted heavily, down on one knee, then suddenly threw his hand out to try and grab the Druid, shouting "Never!"

He did not manage to reach him though, for Hartspell was too quick, and Spiny had now seen an opportunity to enter the fray himself. A large brown ball unrolled from the shadows to the right of the giant and grabbed the chains of the chandelier, pulling the giant backwards and down to his knees again.

The two now wrestled on the floor and Spiny had somehow contrived to wrap the chains around the giant's throat in an attempt to throttle him. Lokil was too big and strong for Spiny though, and a huge hand reached behind his back and began to squeeze the hedgehog, ignoring the rents to his skin made by the spines.

Séamus feared that Spiny would be crushed. He threw his dagger swiftly into the exposed chest of the kneeling giant, instinctively using his new found skill and strength, as the others advanced with swords drawn to put an end to the contest. The giant released his grip on Spiny, leaving the hedgehog free to complete his task of strangulation, stunned by the small but powerful blow he had just received.

Díarmuid signalled to Spiny not to tighten his grip on the chains anymore for the moment. Lokil looked up now at the prince and his companions, circled about him with swords drawn. Surely now, the giant would quit, there was no way out for him.

But Lokil only laughed. Everyone now looked at the giant and at each other in confusion for a second at this unexpected sound of glee. Then the cause became apparent.

"Ha – Wolfspell. Help me kill these dogs!" he rumbled.

A black-cloaked figure had appeared in the doorway to the fort. The very air seemed to chill.

Hartspell took a sharp intake of breath and made to move forward. Meeshan turned to attack the hooded apparition, being the one closest to the entrance and quickest to react. The giant just continued to laugh.

Then his laughter ceased.

The figure, whoever or whatever it was, had turned its back and disappeared. This was too much for Lokil. "Betrayed!" he screamed.

The giant lurched sideways and once more tried to get back to his feet, swinging his arms at those nearest to him, more furious than ever. This was to be his last attack though. Angus and Chouda slashed at his arms with their swords as he struck. Díarmuid plunged his greatsword into the guts of the giant and Spiny tightened his grip once again, finally choking the life out of the huge tyrant. Before anyone could stop him, the huge hedgehog then lifted his poleaxe from his belt and beheaded Lokil. Blood spurted out from the giant's neck, covering the floor.

"For the forest!" Spiny growled, and then retreated respectfully before Díarmuid, as if fearful of reproach.

But Díarmuid had neither the heart nor the energy to upbraid Spiny for his symbolic gesture of vengeance. After all, the hedgehog had fought bravely and the memory of the badger's skull still weighed heavily upon him.

Díarmuid was back in his home and he took a moment to reflect on memories long past, of his brother and happier times. At that moment, the two centaurs made an appearance at the entrance to the fort.

Crannock and Crellock waited patiently until Díarmuid raised his head to look at them. The others in the fort were busy cleaning weapons, nursing injuries or talking about what had occurred. Séamus sat on the stairs with Hartspell, slumped and exhausted. All eyes were on the centaurs now.

"News, sire," said Crannock.

"A visitor," added Crellock, with a wave of his arm, indicating the doorway where a large black crow, the size of a small boy, hopped in.

"Caw!" he squawked. "I am Grapple, Prince Díarmuid. I have much that you must hear!"

"I'll vouch for him!" roared Spiny excitedly from a corner of the hallway.

"Thank you, Spiny!" said Díarmuid with a glance that told him to hold his tongue. "You are welcome, Grapple. What news do you bring?"

Grapple then told his tale, hopping constantly from one foot to another and stopping to caw on a regular basis. It took a long time and was interrupted by many questions from Díarmuid, and some from Hartspell, but the information obtained was both useful and foreboding.

Grapple told that news of the rout of the cavalry by their party at the border of Dragonsrealm had spread rapidly to allies of Díarmuid. A robin who was friendly to the cause of the prince had seen it. It also seemed that Wolfspell knew of it too, perhaps through the magic in the shield of the cavalry leader, and that he had withdrawn to muster forces away from the rath. Strangely, the giant was not made aware of this marshalling of troops, nor warned that the fort was likely to be attacked.

It seemed that Wolfspell had decided to be rid of the giant and assume power himself, encouraging the giant to hunt in the forest and keep the rath solely for his own use, but guarded by his magic of course. Unaware of events, the giant had returned to Dragonshill after a fruitless expedition amongst the woodland for sport and a live supper. Once engaged in fighting Díarmuid's band, had the giant looked like being triumphant, no doubt the hooded Druid would have appeared to aid him and earn his thanks. As it turned out however, he came merely to be sure Lokil was finished; if he came at all and the image was not just a phantom he had conjured up to use as his eyes.

Wolfspell's forces were formidable. In a short time he had perhaps a thousand to put in the field. He would soon have more if action were not taken quickly. Grapple thought that nearly half that number may arrive to support the Prince and that their best hope was to send this force out to meet Wolfspell, enticing him to fight them on their own ground and trusting to fate.

"The odds are against us, caw, sire. But if we wait, the hooded Druid will swell his forces by more than we, caw, and time he will have. Time to think of a strategy to rob us of the advantage of our lofty perch."

Díarmuid looked at Grapple, then at Hartspell, and finally at Séamus.

"What think you, Séamus, of this advice?" asked Díarmuid at last.

Séamus looked up, somewhat surprised to be asked, then realised that he had indeed been going over the options in his head as Grapple spoke.

He cleared his throat. "I can think of none better. But who are these allies that flock to your cause?" he asked.

"The dwarves for one!" boomed a deep, gravelly voice from the doorway.

Standing between the centaurs was what at first looked like a block of stone. As wide as he was tall, the dwarf that had spoken rested his hands on his two-headed axe, standing feet apart, looking immovable and sure.

"I have a hundred followers, all armed and ready. We will hide underground no more from this tyranny now the Prince has returned!"

"They are all outside already," said Crannock bowing to Díarmuid.

"There are more men and more Blemmyai also," added Crellock, copying the bow.

Díarmuid looked shell-shocked. He had returned to his rath and killed Lokil the giant. Wolfspell and his soldiers still ruled in his kingdom, but now he had an army.

Chapter 18

To Battle

"You are welcome Berling of Nidavellir," said Díarmuid, addressing the dwarf, "for I recognised you though I was but a child when you were last at court here."

Berling bowed stiffly, but did not move or reply, clearly expecting more. Dwarves can be quite prickly, and they demand fine words and ceremony.

"The sons of Solblindi will have free passage in Dragonsrealm and across our borders once more," Díarmuid continued, not losing his touch for diplomacy despite the recent messy conclusion to the fight with Lokil.

"I had not expected such quick support and I envisaged a siege whilst we waited and hoped. This is more than I could have dreamed of and I am grateful. We must arm all the men and Blemmyai that require it from the stores here, set a camp, rest and prepare ourselves for battle tomorrow."

So saying, Díarmuid took his leave seeing that Berling was content. He exited up the stairwell trying to mask his emotion. Chouda and Sourbal immediately went outside to see to the needs of the arriving Blemmyai, whilst Angus and Meeshan did their best to equip the new men.

Hartspell was soon busy outside organising setting up of the camp for so many. The top of the mountain was large and relatively flat, but without the Druid's intervention many a squabble may have broken out. The dwarves did not want to move from the spot that they had already occupied and Spiny had to be persuaded by Hartspell and Angus not to walk straight over the top of them.

Six more centaurs had also arrived and were greeted warmly by Crannock and Crellock. They sadly realised that they would be fighting against many more of their own kind in Wolfspell's forces on the morrow though, which tempered their enthusiasm.

These centaurs brought news that other shape-changers and the animals that they could convince from the forest would also come to help. They would not leave their cover for the mountain camp at the moment, but could be expected to show at the battle. Crannock and Crellock looked dubious at this information, although Spiny was satisfied with the news and treated it as a certainty. Grapple departed with messages from the hedgehog for the creatures of the forest to guarantee their appearance at the appropriate moment.

"That'll put the wind up 'em!" he laughed gruffly. "They'll pay for every leaf they've disturbed!" he added, shuffling off.

"I hope he's right," said Crannock.

"Yes," agreed Crellock, "there are barely four hundred here in total, not half the forces of Wolfspell as the bird spoke. We need more."

Yet when morning came, no more had come. Below on the Dragon's Plain Wolfspell's forces could be seen for the first time, as light spread over the mountains from the East. Angus did a quick calculation; being one of the most farsighted was apparently another one of his acquired talents in the Otherworld.

"More like twelve hundred," he said to Díarmuid. "Not counting the air force."

Harpies could be seen occasionally taking off in random positions amongst the otherwise well disciplined ranks. There were perhaps twenty of them, though there could well have been twice that number depending on how many were on the wing at any given time. Wolfspell clearly had some control over them after all.

Séamus shuddered at the memory of those creatures. He felt more feverish than ever this morning and had had a very disturbed night despite having a comfortable chamber to himself in the fort.

His dreams were troubled and he constantly thought somebody was trying to enter his room, but he could not move to defend himself, as if he were pinned to the bed. Then he realised it was a dream and forced himself awake, but the door shifted again and he found he was still pinned down, still dreaming.

Now you know that when you have a dream like this, a nightmare we should say, that when you finally do awake for real after many such false dawns, you are not sure for a short while that you are really awake and you doubt your surroundings.

Séamus can be forgiven then for imagining he was still dreaming, and crying out in frustration, when he did wake up to find the door was open and that a seven-foot hedgehog had curled up on the comfortable rug at the end of the bed, a large bloody bag left down beside him. Spiny was in a good humour though and accepted that Séamus had shouted as a result of his dreaming; leaving the room and even apologising for using it in the night, mentioning something about the noise of a hundred dwarves snoring. Séamus lay in bed for a while after that to regain his composure, the memories of the dreams already dissipated and confused. All except one part.

He had dreamed that a large black bird had appeared on the ledge of the window to his room, the shutters having opened themselves to accept it.

"Grapple?" he had asked, sitting up in surprise.

But the bird was of normal size, a raven black as night. Then the bird was gone and a woman stood before him in a dark, sleeveless cloak. Her hair was as black as the raven's, the skin on her bare arms as white as snow, her lips as red as blood, her eyes as green as emeralds.

"You will go to battle tomorrow, Séamus. I am the Morrigu and you have my favour. But you will be victorious only if you remember your strengths. When all seems lost, remember your gift, remember whose kingdom you fight for."

Her voice was deep and enchanting. Séamus wanted to shout, "Let me fight for you!" but she was gone and the raven back in her place flew off from the window, the shutters closing behind it. Then his other dream returned, the door opening, and Séamus could not move.

Séamus puzzled over this one vivid aspect of his dream that remained. Had he really only dreamed it? What was his gift? His newfound strength and accuracy in his left arm with his dagger? His clear thought and instinct in combat?

Somehow he had to bring that to bear in the battle that was to come, to save Díarmuid, for it was his kingdom that he was fighting for.

Séamus took up a position behind Díarmuid with Hartspell as they prepared to move down the mountain to face Wolfspell's army. No one objected to this and though the Druid gave a look of concern at Séamus's feverish brow, he said nothing, perhaps thinking it was the anxiety about the events of the day to come that was making Séamus sweat.

Díarmuid raised his right arm and then lowered it. This was the signal that began the descent, a regimented march of his forces down to the plain to meet Wolfspell. All orders had already been given, each chosen commander knowing where to position the troops allotted to him.

After an hour and a half, they stopped and formed their battle lines. They were still above the plain in broken ground, a shallow but long climb of over three hundred yards for Wolfspell's army to reach them. The hooded Druid could be seen on horseback in front of his troops, his visage shaded, both armies now staring each other in the face.

"What if he doesn't attack?" asked Séamus.

"He'll have to," replied Díarmuid. "Because we are not moving. I will force his hand if necessary. He dare not back away from here, many of his followers may lose heart and think he is afraid."

For a long time however, nobody moved. It seemed like an eternity, although perhaps it was only half an hour. Wolfspell rode around his forces, rearranging some of them, encouraging, or perhaps threatening others, it was too far to tell for sure. But he acted as if he expected an attack and had no intention of making the first move, leading his forces in an uphill charge that would obviously be a disadvantage to them despite their superiority in numbers.

Murmurs started spreading in Díarmuid's ranks amongst the men, the centaurs and Spiny.

"Why don't we hit them now, with speed from above?" said one voice.

"He is riding around moving troops, now is the time to strike whilst they are disorganised," said another.

The Blemmyai said nothing, but exchanged glances as if uncomfortable in their defensive positions. Díarmuid looked uncertain for the first time and Hartspell furrowed his brow and sniffed the air, uneasy and alarmed but not discerning the cause.

"Magic!" he cried at last. "He tries to demoralise us, to goad us into folly!"

This in itself seemed to snap the thread of disharmony that had begun, but the Druid also started to murmur counter spells to shore up morale and defend against unwonted enchantments coming from the enemy. Men and Blemmyai steeled themselves, nodded to each other, and stood firm, confident in Díarmuid's leadership, determined not to falter again.

The Blemmyai were on his left with one or two men, the better archers, all with long bows. They found themselves facing a fearsome cavalry where the mounts were elephants, the riders ogres. On Díarmuid's right were his own cavalry, men and women on horseback and the eight centaurs. They faced a similar mixture of men and centaurs opposite them, but far more centaurs, at least two dozen, armoured and carrying swords. Díarmuid was relieved that they had no chariots to face, perhaps because they had no charioteers. He almost wished for one of his own so he could charge amongst the enemy now, even though there was no time to incorporate them into his battle strategy and he had no charioteer himself to control the horses for him as he would strike from the vehicle.

In the middle were the majority of soldiers on both sides. Men at arms, some in square schiltrons of spearmen, made up most of Wolfspell's army here, heavily armoured and uniformed in red with the wolf's image on their shields.

Díarmuid's middle was similar but far fewer, less heavily armed but bolstered by the presence of Berling and his dwarves. Díarmuid, Séamus, Hartspell and Meeshan were the only mounted troops amongst them. Angus and Spiny were placed on the left edge of this force, closest to the Blemmyai.

"He has tried to goad us with magic. I will try something more direct!" announced Díarmuid.

"Chouda, prepare your archers. Half to hit the elephants, half to disrupt those tidy spearmen in front of me."

Chouda nodded at Díarmuid, then gave an order to Sourbal. Sourbal quickly had the Blemmyai and men amongst them ready to fire, targets selected. He brought down his fist and a hail of arrows arched skywards and came down with deadly accuracy amongst elephants on the flank and foot soldiers in the middle of Wolfspell's army.

Elephants screamed and jostled, ogres struggling with all their might to keep them steady. Men fell and others left their lines so that the centre began to look more like one mass of people. Wolfspell rode around trying to maintain order and calm, determined not to break his lines but to bring Díarmuid down to him.

"Again!" shouted Díarmuid.

More arrows flew; more men, elephants and ogres fell. More disorder came upon Wolfspell's centre and right flank. His cavalry on the left were untouched but many paced around uneasily at the sight of their comrades in disarray, the horses also made afraid from the screams of the elephants.

Wolfspell returned to the centre of his forces and shouted at men to retake their positions. He then let out a roar, a loud feral sound, an enraged human voice but also like a wolf growling.

"Forward!" he howled.

Díarmuid had got what he wanted, so far. The battle had begun.

Chapter 19

Dragon's Plain

You may have played war games at home. Most children do and so do many adults. It is natural and part of human nature to test ourselves in mock battles as war is a reality that has been with us since the beginnings of our time. To be in a real battle though, that is something else.

The confusion, the terror, the bloodshed, the sights of men and beasts horribly wounded and killed – it is not a place that anybody in his or her right mind would choose to be. Professional soldiers perhaps, hardened mercenaries, people fanatically inspired for a cause, these may seek combat, glory even to satisfy some need or sense of purpose. But even they will not leave a battlefield unscathed, the memories of the horror they have participated in will return to them at some time.

For the ordinary conscript, the volunteer doing his or her perceived duty, or for those caught up in the midst of a conflict against their will, the horror is immediate and the effects can be long lasting. Séamus, even with his gifts in the Otherworld, his new skills with weapons, his calm warrior instinct, was overwhelmed initially with the scale of the slaughter. This was something far removed from the skirmish with the cavalry when they had been ambushed.

However, people, like animals, are also by their nature resilient, adaptive and instilled with an inborn instinct for survival. So it was that Séamus recovered himself, fought bravely, and was later able to shut out the more terrible memories, continue his life relatively unaffected, and even go back to playing war games with his friends at school.

You would not have been able to tell him that this would be the case though, as Wolfspell's centre advanced on Díarmuid's. Séamus sat holding the reins tight on Misty his horse, awaiting Díarmuid's word. On his left the Blemmyai fired arrows continuously and frantically as the elephant cavalry closed in on them carrying their cruel ogre masters. On the right, Díarmuid's cavalry had charged downhill to meet a similar but larger force of men and centaurs coming up at them across the upper slopes of Dragon's Plain.

The sight of a centaur charging is impressive and intimidating enough to make you shake and stare in awe, like a rabbit encountering headlights unexpectedly on the road. To see centaurs charging at each other, each committed to his cause, thundering across open ground with weapons in hand, is a sight to chill the blood. They went straight for each other, and they hit each other without slowing; an explosion of arms, lances, swords, teeth and hooves. That either could come out alive seemed impossible, yet one would emerge, bloody and triumphant, his rival still or breathing his last, splayed out on the battlefield at the feet of the victor.

Díarmuid's cavalry did well. The impetus of their downhill charge gave them extra speed, a shock to the uniformed forces of Wolfspell. The latter too fought more like the reluctant conscript, for survival mostly, whereas Díarmuid's men were fighting for their Prince and their future as well as for the present.

The centaurs fighting for Díarmuid had the advantage also of riding armed with lances and swords from the armoury in the fort, whereas Wolfspell's centaurs were armed like the rest of his cavalry, with swords and shields. Using the lance was more natural for a centaur in a charging attack, the extra length making close control less necessary, so Díarmuid's centaurs frequently got the first blow in and had the greater success.

Inevitably though, numbers told, and a force of thirty or more, mostly men with one or two centaurs, broke through and threatened the side of Díarmuid's infantry. Díarmuid with Meeshan, Hartspell and Séamus rode to intercept them with ten pike men and a dozen dwarves dispatched by their commanders to support them and block the attack.

On Díarmuid's command at the same time, his centre forces moved forward to meet the first of the phalanxes that had struggled up the slope to engage them. Men and dwarves spilled forward from their defences with shouts and oaths, Angus and Spiny and a few of the Blemmyai amongst them.

Whilst awaiting the frontal assault, Séamus had noticed Meeshan calmly taking a number of small pots from her backpack, like little earthenware jars the size of a clenched fist, with a taper at the top as with a candle. They appeared to be in two parts that connected together which Meeshan separated, filling the hollow inside with the contents of a small bag – tiny multi-coloured and multi-edged crystals. When she had reconnected the top of the pot, she proceeded to pour a dark liquid from a long bottle into a small hole from which she had temporarily removed the taper. It suddenly occurred to Séamus that she was making primitive hand-grenades, and he wondered how she would prime or ignite them. Surely she didn't have a box of matches?

By the time they had turned to meet the flanking sortie of Wolfspell's cavalry, Meeshan had completed six of these and she had attached them to the saddle of her horse, which Séamus noticed for the first time contained a number of small pockets around the edges. His question was then very soon answered.

Releasing her reins as she rode expertly forward, Meeshan seized two of her pots and skilfully scraped the tops of them together in a firm, swift movement. The surface around the taper on the pots contained a rough, marble-like, stone which instantly sparked vigorously with the friction, igniting the tapers that had soaked up some of the oil inside. In the same movement the grenades were thrown, one from each hand,

and then her sword and shield appeared in their stead a second later.

The effect was devastating. No man, horse or centaur were seriously injured or killed by the explosions, but the flash of light and smoke and the numerous small fragments of glass and hard clay from the exploded pot did enough to knock several to the ground with numerous cuts and simultaneously terrify several more into bolting. The numbers now favoured the small force with Díarmuid that had been despatched to meet the riders, though most of these were on foot.

On the other flank, the Blemmyai's arrows had effectively halted the elephant charge. One or two reached them and caused mayhem for a short time, but enough Blemmyai with spears drove them off. Most of the ogres that had not fled had been forced to meet the Blemmyai dismounted, and the numbers there were now reasonably even also. The ogres were far larger and more powerful, but they were less adroit and less intelligent. The Blemmyai standing slightly uphill from them held their own and the casualties were not as one-sided as might have been imagined. With Sourbal conducting operations whilst he fought and Chouda showing the strength and skill for which he had been elected leader, the left flank at least was secure.

The main force was in the centre though, and here things were starting to go badly for Díarmuid. The initial charge into the first phalanxes had gone well. The dwarves were sturdy fighters, the men well disciplined and eager. Spiny and Angus amongst them, they had ripped through Wolfspell's front lines as if they could not be stopped. But the next line slowed them down and momentum was lost. They were now fighting amongst a far superior number and in danger of being surrounded. The armour of the enemy was strong and as the battle progressed it seemed to become more impregnable. Angus noticed that Wolfspell from behind the lines was chanting and casting spells over his army and guessed the extra protection on top of the armour came from that source. There was nothing he could do about it though. Even Spiny, on his hind feet and wielding his poleaxe, looked like he may soon be overrun with foes, a pike getting past his defences once already and marking his white soft belly with an expanding streak of red. Harpies from above were picking off more and more men. Several of the flying monsters had been downed by Blemmyai bows on Sourbal's instructions, before the ogres arrived to force them to close combat. But many remained, cravenly selecting the weakest or most isolated opponents, sometimes in pairs.

It was then that the animals arrived. Some were larger than usual, shape-changers like Spiny, Séamus assumed. Most were normal creatures of the woods – bears, boars, badgers, foxes and even hares. They were following the larger of the animals as if following orders and came from behind on all sides. A raven flew overhead screeching as if imploring all to do great deeds in battle and indeed this seemed to drive the animals on to further efforts. The remnants of Wolfspell's cavalry on both flanks were now dispersed.

Many animals died in the assault, but the Blemmyai and the remaining cavalry of Díarmuid were now free to enter the fray in the centre of the battlefield where the day would be won or lost. Eagles, falcons, crows, gulls and a variety of smaller birds had also arrived with Grapple. The Harpies were their targets and they were forced to flee under a sustained and ferocious attack.

But there was less success for the animals that had attacked Wolfspell's centre. Spearmen, Harpies and a blast of wind that emanated from the hooded magician himself had quickly driven these off.

Now the battle was concentrated into one mass on Dragon's Plain and the remaining animals also dispersed. It was as if, their job done, they had returned to being the normal cautious creatures of the forest and followed their natural instinct of flight. Soon, it was as if they had never been there at all, apart from two creatures that remained, a massive bear and an equally over-sized fox. These fought their way through to where Spiny stood and joined him, the three back to back making a pile of bodies around them. The animals and birds had done all that could have been asked of them though, yet it seemed that it might not be enough.

Hartspell had been at liberty, once Wolfspell's cavalry were routed, to cast spells of protection over Díarmuid's forces and to attempt to counter the spells of Wolfspell. This was all he could effectively do however; negate the other Druid. What was left was a melee in which the odds had been reduced from three-to-one to two-to-one. The advantage of bowmen and higher ground had gone in the close combat, and the greater numbers of Wolfspell's force now surely had the upper hand. Despite early successes, the defeat of the enemy cavalry, the assistance of the forest creatures, Díarmuid's army was in dire trouble.

Wolfspell's army seemed to realise the position and sense victory. They fought bravely and determinedly to bring their advantage to bear. Séamus, fighting on the fringes, exhausted and more feverish than ever, could clearly see the predicament. He drove his opponent back but then got jostled over by two men fighting each other near him. He rolled backwards and clear of the battle for a moment, propped up against a rock, breathing heavily and seemingly unnoticed or ignored by those a few yards in front of him. He looked up and saw the only birds in the sky now were carrion, not fighting for anybody, just waiting to feed.

Then a raven landed on another stone near to him, cocked a head sideways and gave him a hard stare.

The Morrigu, thought Séamus, and he remembered his dream. He looked again and the bird had gone. Calmly and slowly, he climbed up the slope and stood back to view the battle before and below him. He saw Spiny, separated from his forest companions rolling in a ball in the direction of the hooded Druid. Hartspell and Díarmuid with Chouda, Sourbal and Angus were cutting a sway behind him. They had realised the predicament and decided that a small group should launch a desperate attack on Wolfspell. If they could kill him, would his troops still fight? Séamus could see that it was the only option left open to them, but they had a long way to go to get to the Druid.

Then explosions cleared more of a path in front of the advancing hedgehog. Meeshan had used the remainder of her grenades. She must have managed somehow to bring them with her as she was forced to fight on foot in the chaotic scenes of slaughter, that were played out like a *danse macabre* in front of Séamus.

Wolfspell noticed the danger instantly. Another fierce wind emanated from him and stopped Spiny in his tracks. The assault party following him were also stopped and the gap created by Meeshan was being closed in again by enemy troops. Hartspell seemed unable to prevent the effects of the wind and the last desperate bid looked like it would fail.

Séamus felt himself grabbing his dagger. They were the other side of the battlefield, three hundred yards or more away. He couldn't possibly, could he? But he had to save Díarmuid to win the day. That was what the dream meant wasn't it?

As if building up power, Séamus slowly pulled his arm back, steadied himself and released the dagger with every ounce of energy he had. The light from the sundial blazed enough to dazzle him for a moment and he fell back.

He heard the scream, almost felt it. Wolfspell's spell was broken; a dagger was buried to the hilt in his left shoulder. With his right hand the hooded Druid removed the weapon, collapsing in pain as he did so.

Hartspell, who had at last managed to move himself alone in the face of the gale, advanced towards him. His companions were no longer in the grip of the unnatural wind, but once more had a crowd of soldiers to overcome if they were to break through to assist their Druid.

Angus attacked particularly furiously as if enraged by his impotence in the face of Wolfspell's gale. He had been unaffected by any demoralising spells of the hooded Druid, Meeshan had been correct about his immunity to such magic. He could do nothing however about magic that was not directed at him in particular, like the gale or the protection spells over Wolfspell's troops. He abandoned his targe, or small shield, and from the fold in his plaid above his waist produced a small dagger, a *skian dhu*. Nowadays this is worn in the sock of ceremonial highland dress, but in reality it was a concealed weapon, brought quickly and easily to hand. With his claymore and his dagger, he fought like a whirling dervish, a berserker impervious to harm. It looked as though he may break through to assist Hartspell, but then suddenly more soldiers arrived between him and the two Druids, and the chance was gone. He now, like the others, was merely fighting for his life.

Wolfspell arose, his teeth gritted, his eyes ablaze, the hood fallen from his head to reveal a dark-haired, swarthy young man. He was handsome and muscular, having more the appearance of a king's champion than of a Druid.

"You are able to raise a wind almost as well as my old friend Stormspell," said Hartspell dispassionately, taking another step towards his fellow magician.

"That old dotard!" spat Wolfspell. "He told me all I needed to know about this little princedom and I learned all his magic – it didn't take long!"

"Then he deceived you," replied Hartspell, smiling. "There is much you could have learned from him."

"I doubt that," Wolfspell grinned in return, "but I can always visit his dungeon in the Ice Mountains and see if you speak the truth."

Hartspell nodded grimly as if he had just heard confirmed what he had suspected all along.

"You will not get the chance," he said.

An instant later, in a flurry of arms, he dropped his staff and his sword and where he had stood was a massive stag, a white hart with red ears and sharp, heavy antlers. His head was down, charging immediately, and Wolfspell seemed certain to be impaled.

Just as suddenly though, the young Druid was gone. A wolf, equally large, with a seemingly oversized head, full of razor sharp teeth, dodged the antlers and slashed at the hart with cruel claws. Both creatures were injured in the initial collision, and now they circled each other, looking for an opening for another attack, each determined to see an end to their foe.

Séamus saw all this from his vantage point on the slope of the plain. His friends were isolated at the rear of the conflict now, the two Druids battling behind them. The rest of Díarmuid's forces had regrouped away to his left, retreating up the slope away from the pursuing forces of Wolfspell, their victory now seemingly assured.

He had remembered his dream, tried to save Díarmuid, thrown his dagger with all his heart and skill, but to no avail. He had only injured Wolfspell, and the Druid had quickly healed himself of that hurt. Hartspell might defeat the wolf, but that was hardly a certainty against his younger opponent. It would all take time anyway. By then his friends, Díarmuid included, must surely have fallen; the rest of Díarmuid's army would have been put to flight to be hunted down at leisure. There was nothing more that he could do.

The fever was so strong now from the Harpy's poison that Séamus felt he could not move, all he could do was watch the end. The enemy would find him eventually, he was hardly hidden, and it would all be over. He wondered what people would think when he failed to return to the Tavern. Would his sister guess what had happened?

Thinking of her, he remembered her pushing the brooch into his hand and he clasped it against his chest. It was a gift certainly and she had thought it important to give it to him. His head suddenly span with new possibilities, possibilities that may never have occurred to him had he not been so feverish.

"When all seems lost, remember your gift, remember whose kingdom you fight for." That was what the Morrigu had said. That was what the raven had wanted him to do. The brooch was the gift, the image of the dragon encircled devouring its own tail. This was Dragonsrealm. Díarmuid had said he would only ever be a Prince here; the dragon was the King. They were fighting for the Dragon's Kingdom.

As the realisation grew, Séamus felt the power in the brooch as it shone silver through his fingers. It was far brighter and clearer than any glow from the sundial motif on his wrist; the light seemed to engulf him as he spoke, hardly aware of what he was saying.

The earth shook. Séamus was summoning the dragon.

Chapter 20

Prince Díarmuid's Inheritance

Instinctively, both armies separated, backing away from each other at the main line of battle and ceasing hostilities. At the rear, where Díarmuid and his small band of followers had attempted the assault on Wolfspell, the surrounded party also got a sudden respite. The hart and the wolf stood their ground but made no further attempt on each other. All looked about them and at each other, trying to keep their feet on the trembling ground.

In his mind's eye, Séamus pictured a dragon emerging and attacking Wolfspell's men, the soldiers in the red cloaks with the wolf's head on their shields, his own companions remaining untouched. Whether guided by this unspoken instruction, or whether it was purely coincidence, the ground opened beneath the main body of Wolfspell's force, flames leaping up from the fissures.

Now there was pandemonium. Men and beasts screamed; those not immediately swallowed up scrambled to try to get to safety as the earth shifted and flames licked around them. Díarmuid's main force was mostly untouched, though some at the front of the ranks had fallen, and they now retreated further up the hill away from the broken ground, no longer the level plain. Díarmuid rallied his small force at the rear, so far also unaffected by the fissures, ensuring they were ready for any new onslaught.

There was little chance of that though. Even here, there was panic. They had seen the main body of their army swallowed up, attacked by the very ground beneath their feet, and they were in disarray. Suddenly, the feral scream of Wolfspell could be heard again.

Angus was upon him, planting his *skian dhu* heavily in the creature's chest. No one had seen the scout move when the earth tremors began, but he had left Díarmuid's group and sneaked right up to the mighty wolf as if invisible. In defence, the wolf had managed to kick Angus backwards with his hind legs, but it seemed that the determined Free Knight would surely finish the job with his claymore on the next strike.

In an instant though, Wolfspell was back in human form, and another gale whipped up around him, carrying the bleeding Druid away from the plain at speed, as if he were flying. With a curse, Angus was running with impossible speed over the edge of the plain after him, trying to keep pace with the wind, and remarkably not losing too much ground.

Hartspell, also returned once more to his human form, watched the two figures disappear, and then returned his gaze to what had been the battlefield.

Wolfspell's army was defeated, but the earth continued to shake, and new fissures sprang up as if randomly, endangering all. Huge towers of rock pushed up from beneath the surface like giant teeth, flames exploded out of gullies, and the intensity of the tremors increased with every heartbeat.

With a quick incantation, Hartspell was now up in the air. He went floating on a small white cloud across the plain, easily but quickly, towards the lonely figure of Séamus, still sitting eyes closed, his blazing dragon-brooch clenched tightly in his fist. The Druid landed hastily besides him and grabbed his shoulder, speaking urgently, alarmed at the burning fever now clearly etched on Séamus's features.

"Séamus! You must stop! You must! You cannot control this creature. It will devour the world and itself! Release it to slumber once more! Séamus!"

The Druid had to shout over the tumult of the earthquake and the sounds of men fighting for their lives.

Through his fever Séamus heard the Druid's voice, but what was it that he should stop? He was saving his friends, doing what the Morrigu had told him, using his sister's gift. The image of the raven and Sinéad came into his mind again, the Druid's voice strangely incongruous with their faces.

He heard the Druid say, "You cannot control this creature." Then, it was the voice of the Morrigu saying, "It will devour the world and itself!" Then, the voice changed once more, and it was his sister speaking, "Release it to slumber once more!"

Release? He was holding the dragon-brooch that his sister had given him. He had summoned the dragon – that was it. And now he must let go. With an effort, he slackened his grip and opened his eyes. He saw Hartspell staring down at him frantically, shouting "Séamus!" The light went out and the brooch was dull. The tremors subsided and the flames ceased. Then Séamus passed out.

*

Díarmuid was beside Séamus when he reawakened. He was back in the same chamber within Díarmuid's rath that he had slept in the night before. It seemed the fever had been burned out of him by the fire within the brooch or by his own inner strength. Everything came back to him clearly now, and he sat bolt upright.

"The battle! The dragon! What—"

"Peace, Séamus," interrupted Díarmuid, holding up a hand to silence his friend as he had done more than once before.

"The battle is over, Dragonsrealm is mine to rule once more. Our King sleeps beneath us again and will not awake until the end of the world."

From the shadows in the corner of the room, a huge shape shambled forward and stuck its nose above the sheets next to Díarmuid.

"Sorry, your majesty!" said Spiny. "Had to see how the Champion was for myself."

Séamus's mouth formed the question, looking at Díarmuid.

"Yes, Séamus," said the Prince. "It was unanimously decided that you would be my Champion, seeing as you won the day." He held up his hand again to prevent another interruption.

"I know you want to get home and you won't be staying. Another will perform your duties in your absence, but the honour is yours. Accept it, you deserve it."

"I, I... thank you. What of the others? Is anybody hurt?"

"All are hurt, Séamus, but wounds will heal. I'm afraid we lost many men at arms, including Chouda, Emer and Spiny's companion from the forest, Swiftpad the great fox."

"He was some fighter!" bellowed Spiny, getting up onto his hind legs in tribute, tears in his eyes.

"Yes, Spiny, he was," sighed Díarmuid, carefully patting the hedgehog on the side. "None will be forgotten. Now, let's leave the Champion to get some rest, eh?"

The two retreated from the room, gently closing the door behind them, leaving Séamus alone once more. He lay back in his bed again, tears now falling from his eyes for the loss of his companions and for the terrible sights he had seen on the battlefield that day. He had done what he had to do, but how many men's deaths had been caused when he summoned the dragon? Had the young Emer died because of it, or had she lost her life fighting Wolfspell's forces? How old had she been?

He slept uneasily through the afternoon until Hartspell, who asked him to attend the banquet downstairs, visited him. It was a banquet to celebrate victory, the return of the Prince, the banishing of the Giant and tyranny, and to remember fallen comrades.

He counselled and comforted Séamus with many words as Séamus dressed and prepared himself. He spoke on the futility of regret for actions that could not have been avoided. He spoke of the necessity of moving on from sorrow, for self-preservation and peace of mind, though never forgetting and always learning. And he spoke of life containing many battles, in one form or another, sometimes with yourself, sometimes with others, sometimes with nature itself.

"We hope to be at peace for the greater part of our existence, but the battles must be faced. Life is to be relished, victory or defeat in each battle an experience towards our greater enlightenment."

"But all must fall eventually," he continued. "It is the cycle of life. But if you act as you have done, with courage, dignity, love and consideration for others; when the time comes that you must fall yourself, then you will be content, not sorry."

"Come now," he added after a pause. "We will enjoy the banquet!"

During the course of the evening, Séamus was knighted by Prince Díarmuid and bestowed with the title of Champion of Dragonsrealm. The six of the original group of twelve that had joined Díarmuid and survived the campaign were also knighted and made part of an honorary guard. These were Brannan, Dafydd, Cliona, Corey, Cormac and Niall.

Hartspell agreed to help out as a Druid in the princedom until a replacement was found, but insisted that he must return shortly to his own country.

Spiny was made guardian of the forest and ambassador for the creatures within it. Séamus had to suppress a smile at the thought of the abrasive hedgehog acting as a diplomat.

Then pledges of friendship and alliance were traded with the dwarves who were present, each managing to eat as much if not more than their taller fellow guests. A pardon was also given to men, centaurs and other beasts that had fought for Lokil or Wolfspell, the new reign to begin for all subjects free from fears and recriminations.

Séamus also learned about the fate of Angus, last seen chasing Wolfspell from the Dragon's Plain. Meeshan, still with a healthy contempt for her fellow Free Knight, speculated that he had been working on a commission to kill Wolfspell and merely used Díarmuid's campaign for his own ends to get to the Druid.

Initially, Díarmuid was angry with this, but Hartspell reminded him that Angus had done nothing but assist in the Prince's cause and that they had had excellent service from him. Díarmuid had to agree that this was so and promised to reward the scout should he return, though he said he would make it his business if he did so to find out who he had been working for, and whether, specifically, it had been Lokil the giant.

Séamus also noticed that Meeshan's role and her reward were not discussed. Díarmuid for now was content to have her sat beside him, radiant in flowing gowns from the rath's own wardrobes, enjoying her company as much as she seemed to enjoy his. He wondered at this whether Díarmuid had inherited more than he had bargained for.

*

The next morning, Hartspell, Díarmuid, Meeshan and Spiny accompanied Séamus to the forest beyond the plains. A small unit of cavalry came with them also, just in case any people were still loyal to Lokil and Wolfspell, though it was apparent that all loyalty for the former regime had quickly drained away, as if a spell had been broken. The word had also spread of the pardon and amnesty, and even if some may not have believed it, they could wait and see what would occur, and they saw no immediate need to take up arms once more.

The cavalry were ordered to stop at the edge of the forest as the others entered. This was where the passage, the source of power that would lead Séamus back to his own world, was said to be. Hartspell knew of the cave and Spiny was able to confirm its existence and its location, stating that it was known as a place where no animal would set foot, and was forbidden to the shape-shifters.

"But what do I do?" asked Séamus, bewildered for the moment.

"Just enter," said Hartspell. "Picture yourself back in your own world at the time that you left. You have the power and ability to make the journey. Díarmuid spotted it before, and he was right wasn't he?"

Díarmuid looked at Séamus and nodded agreement and encouragement.

"Goodbye, Séamus," he said. "And good luck!"

Séamus dismounted from Misty and gave her a fond farewell pat. He walked to the cave, turned once and waved to his companions. Then he entered.

It was very dark, and he had to feel his way along the walls of the cavern, not sure where he was putting his feet.

He concentrated as best he could on returning home, but he just seemed to be walking further and further in. How big was this cave? It was now getting noticeably colder as well, as if a fog had enveloped him, and Séamus was breathing heavily. Then the cave collapsed.

Scrambling through the rocks and dirt, Séamus tried desperately to come up for air, flailing his arms around in the debris. His head came out at last, followed by his body, but not back into darkness.

It took him a while to find his bearings. He could hear the sea. He was covered in sand, not dust or dirt from the cave. It was late afternoon, and it was turning into a dark November evening.

He was on Bertra strand, hidden amongst the dunes, two miles or so from the car park at the Reek. The beach was deserted apart from a couple walking a dog, who looked up surprised and disapprovingly at the boy who they noticed in the dunes. Because of erosion, a polite notice asked people to keep off that area of the beach.

Séamus waved apologetically and scrambled down to the flat sand. He noticed his watch was back on his left wrist, and then that he was back in his usual clothes. It said six o'clock. Shaking sand from his hair, looking up at the imposing view of Croagh Patrick and the rising moon, he began to run. It was time he was back in the Tavern, and it was beginning to rain.

Epilogue

Back to Reality

Séamus arrived in good time at the Tavern, out of breath, to find his grandfather in no hurry to leave. Fortunately, he had only had one pint when he had arrived, making it last a while before having two cups of coffee as the meeting progressed.

He knew he would have to drive Séamus home earlier than normal, that is before closing time, as Séamus's father would be returning on the train late in the evening. Mrs Moran would want to get all jobs out of the way before then, including feeding the children and getting them cleaned up. On another day, Séamus would have had to wait a while for his grandfather to order a taxi and for it to come, but Séamus's arrival galvanised his grandfather into action and within twenty minutes they were on the road.

His grandfather was in good form after seeing his friends and didn't raise an eyebrow when Séamus had said, in response to a polite question about Séamus's time on the Reek, that he had decided to walk up to Bertra strand. He had said this because he thought Granddad would notice sand present on his clothes and shoes, but he need not have worried. Granddad was still going over jokes and conversations in the pub from the afternoon and hardly noticed what Séamus said at all.

By nine thirty both Séamus and Sinéad were bathed, fed and watered. They enjoyed Friday evenings, not only because they stayed up a bit later, but also because they looked forward to meeting their father on the train from Dublin, seeing him arrive before a short weekend, after which he would soon depart again Sunday evening or sometimes Monday morning.

It had all been a rush of activity in the Moran household after Séamus returned, so Sinéad had not had a chance to quiz him, though Séamus sensed by her look that she had a thousand questions lined up. Still, the talk in the car on the way to Westport station was all about Daddy and what they would do at the weekend before school resumed on Monday.

They both rushed to meet him when they saw he had got off the train, having had to walk to the front of the train from his seat at the rear to get off on the short platform, and then having to find a way past a confusion of elderly ladies.

"Hello Séamus! Sinéad! How was your half-term?" he asked.

"Fine, lovely. Great to see you, Daddy!" said Sinéad.

"Oh, the usual," said Séamus with a grin.

There was something about the way he said it and Sinéad's conspiratorial smile that made him look at Séamus questioningly for a moment. Then he smiled and tussled his hair.

"I bet," he said. Then he added, "Is that sand?"

Mrs Moran then caught up with them and they headed back to the car, the two adults deep in conversation. This carried on during the journey home, and finally Sinéad turned to Séamus in the back and whispered to him.

"So, it all went okay then?"

"Yes. Thanks, Sinéad," said Séamus, fishing out the brooch from his trouser pocket to hand back to her. It was still shiny as it had been in the Otherworld.

"No, I think that was always meant for you," said Sinéad, closing his opened hand around it again. "That was obvious once Johnny the Pookie turned up!"

Séamus nodded in agreement, though he didn't know how or where she got her ideas and her information. He was just glad now that she did.

"Or should I say Díarmuid?" she added, with a mischievous smile.

It took a moment, and then Séamus turned towards her, his brow furrowed.

"But how can you possibly know that?" he demanded.

Sinéad's smile faded for a second, and she looked a little concerned.

"I was talking to his sister. In a dream that is. I'll tell you about it later."